# Angie's First Case

**Other APPLE PAPERBACKS
You Will Want to Read**

*Casey and the Great Idea*
    by Joan Lowery Nixon
*Encyclopedia Brown and the
Case of the Dead Eagles*
    by Donald J. Sobol
*Encyclopedia Brown Carries On*
    by Donald J. Sobol
*Kid Power*
    by Susan Beth Pfeffer
*The Magic Moscow*
    by Daniel M. Pinkwater
*The Revenge of the Incredible Dr. Rancid
and His Youthful Assistant, Jeffrey*
    by Ellen Conford
*Wally*
    by Judie Wolkoff

# Angie's First Case

by
**Donald J. Sobol**

Illustrated by
**Gail Owens**

---
AN
**APPLE**
PAPERBACK
---

SCHOLASTIC BOOK SERVICES
New York Toronto London Auckland Sydney Tokyo

12 11 10 9 8 7 6 5 4 3 2                    3 4 5 6/8
                Printed in the U.S.A.                11

*for Patricia Slack*

# Chapter
# 1

It was a fine day for hunting the Wolfpack, Angie told herself as she closed the front door and started jogging down Rock Garden Lane. She drew a few deep breaths, quickly found her pace, and struck out purposefully for Seaward Island.

The July air was clean, with a slight tang of ocean salt. It was a few minutes before ten o'clock. Within an hour the Florida sun would take command, and it would be too hot for jogging and too late for spying. By eleven o'clock, the Wolfpack was always done.

Angie turned onto Sixty-eighth Street, keeping alert for anything suspicious.

The Wolfpack was the name the *Dadesville Journal* had given a gang of cocky teen-age thieves. Since Christmas, they had broken into a dozen homes in the city. They chose the hour between ten and eleven o'clock in the morning, after the jobholders had left for work. They stole expensive electronic equipment and jewelry.

The *Journal* had picked up on the gang because they enjoyed taunting the police. After each robbery, a member would telephone headquarters to give the address of the home they had broken into and boast of what had been stolen.

Jogging had been Angie's idea. What better cover for scouting the neighborhoods of Dadesville? The Wolfpack would never suspect a jogging twelve-year-old girl of hunting them.

"Don't be a hero," Kit, her older sister, had cautioned. "Jot down the license plate number and a description of the vehicle they use. Then get to a telephone."

Angie had promised. But she wondered how she would react to danger. Would she really be able to act cautiously?

She wasn't fooling herself. She knew Kit didn't believe the hunt would come to anything — certainly not real danger. Otherwise Kit, who was a police officer, would never have permitted it.

So far, Kit's judgment had proved correct. Since school had let out for the summer three weeks ago, Angie had jogged every morning. Three weeks, and not even a clue.

Yet every morning she had left the house with fresh determination. This morning would be *the* morning.

Her legs were working powerfully. Up and down they pumped, chubby, tough, tireless. She hated them. She wished she were built like Kit, a six-footer, whose long, feather-footed strides ate up the miles.

For a few yards, Angie attempted to bring her feet down lightly. No use. She felt as graceful as an ostrich.

As she approached Edgemore Drive, an empty station wagon came into view. It was parked, with one door open to the curb, in front of a white house. The engine was running.

Angie pretended to labor as she jogged by. Just beyond the rear bumper, she halted and pulled out her handkerchief to wipe her face.

As the handkerchief unfolded, ten pennies dropped out. The trick was surefire. It allowed her to stay in one place and observe. No one could suspect her of being concerned with anything but picking up the pennies.

The door of the white house opened. A man stepped out, fumbling to close his briefcase. A woman appeared behind him and called: "Harry!"

The man spun, kissed her cheek, and hurried out to the station wagon. "If my head weren't fastened on, I'd forget it, too," he shouted. With a wave to the woman, he drove off.

False alarm.

Since Angie had been hunting the Wolfpack, false alarms had become as much a way of life as stinging lungs and aching leg muscles.

She was picking up the pennies when Jess Berg hailed her.

"If you're going to Seaward Island, don't bother," he said, not unpleasantly.

He was sitting on his front stoop. Around his neck hung a pair of binoculars.

"They're widening the Sixty-eighth Street Bridge," he explained. "You'll have to go by the Whitehorse."

The Whitehorse Bridge was at the southern tip of Seaward Island, about three miles away.

Angie hesitated, wondering if Jess was teasing her. She decided to see for herself.

She followed Sixty-eighth Street five more blocks and came upon the construction. Big yellow machines growled and gouged and scraped. Two policemen detoured traffic to the right and left.

Returning to Jess, she flopped down beside him on the stoop.

"Next time you'll believe me," he said.

"I wouldn't believe you if you swore you were alive," Angie tossed back. She slapped her knee in exasperation. "I had a hunch something was going to happen on Seaward Island today."

"Something important?"

"Never mind."

He peered at her. "You're all sweaty, you know. Girls shouldn't sweat. Makes 'em look like a shower cap."

"Climb back into your jar," Angie retorted. She

4

jabbed at the binoculars. "What's with those?"

"I'm bird-watching," Jess said. "And thinking about the poor farmers in Sacramento. They grew twenty-five tons of onions too big for hamburger buns."

Angie struggled to keep from smiling.

She liked Jess Berg. He'd been in her class the last two years, and he usually aced the tests. She had liked him right off. Only she wished they could talk instead of just teasing each other.

From the corner of her eye she saw a blue car coming in their direction. It stopped far up the block on Sixty-eighth Street. Something about the car seized her attention. She shifted around, half expecting the Wolfpack to pile out.

Instead, a man in a tan suit emerged. He pulled out a black suitcase and walked toward Angie and Jess.

In the middle of the block, he went up to the door of a stone house. Apparently no one was at home. The man moved along the street, stopping at several doors. None opened for him.

Angie glanced at her wristwatch. It was 10:23.

"Playing cop again?" Jess asked.

"None of your business."

"One cop in the family ought to be enough," Jess said. "Two, and a guest couldn't bring over a fast-food order without getting a speeding ticket."

Angie wrinkled her nose and held her gaze on the man in the tan suit.

He had stopped at a house nearly opposite them.

5

Angie could see a woman near a second-floor window. She wore an orange robe and was arranging books.

The man's right hand went to the doorbell. The woman upstairs did not respond. After a minute, the man walked on.

"He's probably selling something," Jess remarked.

"He's acting very strange," Angie muttered.

Jess let the comment pass. He seemed to be enjoying watching Angie watch the man.

The man ignored the next two houses. He went up to the third and pressed the doorbell.

When the door swung open, the man drew back a step as if surprised. A big soldier filled the doorway.

Angie couldn't hear what was said, but the big soldier seemed puzzled. He shook his head and gestured. The man in the tan suit picked up his suitcase and retreated.

"Sergeant Casey must have got a long weekend pass," Jess said. "He usually leaves early Monday for the Homestead Air Force Base."

The man in the tan suit walked rapidly back to his car, not bothering with the rest of the houses on the block. As soon as he was behind the wheel, the engine roared.

Instead of continuing down the street toward Angie and Jess, the car made a U-turn, tires screeching.

6

"Quick, get his license number!" cried Angie.

Jess clapped the binoculars to his eyes. "Florida . . . AT forty-one, seventeen. Five-year-old Chevy two-door. Dents in the right rear fender. Blue repaint job."

"You're pretty good," conceded Angie.

"I have *two* hobbies," Jess said. "Birds and cars."

"Combine the two," suggested Angie. "You might help the energy crisis. A car that runs on feathers."

"Maybe next year," Jess said. "Right now I'm crossing parrots with carrier pigeons, so you can send talking messages."

Angie chuckled, though it meant losing ground. The game was never to let Jess know he had topped her.

He was looking at her attentively.

"We — we could go for a walk on the beach," he said.

Angie was taken unprepared. "Sounds okay," she managed.

With the Sixty-eighth Street Bridge closed, she could do no more about Seaward Island and the Wolfpack today. Besides, it was almost eleven o'clock.

"I've got my allowance," Jess said. "We could eat lunch at Bill's Bar-B-Q."

"I like ribs," Angie said.

Jess got to his feet. "Let's go," he commanded.

7

Angie didn't mind. Boys grew bossy when unsure of themselves.

He took her hand.

Suddenly the morning wasn't a waste. Jess was more fun than anybody, and he might even help her track down the Wolfpack. Those binoculars could be useful.

*He didn't mean the remark about sweating,* she thought. Her hand was slippery wet, but he hadn't let go.

"You won't play cop any more today?" he asked.

"I'm off duty."

As they strolled toward the beach, Angie thought once, briefly, about the man in the tan suit. She felt pretty sure he was a suspect. All she had to do was discover his crime.

# Chapter

## 2

When Angie returned from the beach it was nearly five o'clock. Aunt Velma sat in the living room with the evening newspaper.

A short, spare woman of forty-three, Aunt Velma had a ready smile and a belief in clear thinking and plain talking. She closed the newspaper as Angie leaned to kiss her.

"Have a good day?"

"Yes," answered Angie. "Jess Berg and I went to the beach. What's for dinner?"

"When Kit gets home, we'll see. We might run out for a bite. And while we're on the subject, your nose looks like a French fry."

"It doesn't hurt," Angie said.

"There's some zinc ointment in the bathroom."

It was not a command. Aunt Velma never commanded. She made suggestions or presented facts.

For example, she would never *tell* Angie to tidy up her room. Instead, she would state firmly: "Angie, your room looks like a zoo again."

Angie found the tube of zinc ointment in the bathroom medicine cabinet. She smeared the stuff on her nose gingerly.

As she worked it in, the zinc ointment changed to gooey mud. Suddenly she wasn't Angie Zane, hunter of the Wolfpack. She was Lieutenant Angie Zane, World War II commando, darkening her face beneath a black stocking cap.

*No time for regrets now, or for thinking of the past. At 0500 hours she would be parachuting into Nazi-held France. Chin up!*

Angie's mind was a secret hiding place from boredom and disappointment, a wonderland where anything was possible, where she could be anywhere and anyone, and where — since Kit had joined the police force — she could even create and solve her own mysteries. "Angie," Aunt Velma was fond of saying, "you can heighten a sneeze into a drama."

*The green light flashed and she jumped. Tracer bullets sizzled around her even as the parachute opened and followed her down.*

The front door slammed. The land behind the Germans' beach defenses puffed apart at the sound of Kit's voice.

The two sisters had a pact. Angie wouldn't pester Kit about the day's crimes — right away.

10

After eight hours in a patrol car, Kit wanted time to relax. But once she was rested, she would tell Angie everything.

Lately, the pact had been especially hard on Angie. It meant that when Kit came home each evening, she had to swallow the big question: Had the Wolfpack struck again?

Kit walked out of the living room, remarking to Aunt Velma about an easy day. In her left hand she carried her briefcase. Her right held the gun belt.

She stooped, kissed Angie, and strode into her room. Angie fell in close behind and sat down on the bed. She watched silently as the tall figure in the brown police uniform unlocked the top drawer of her dresser.

Kit paused before opening the drawer. Her gaze touched the photographs of their parents on top of the dresser. Angie often saw that look; it said the man and woman were not forgotten.

They had died together in an automobile accident ten years ago. Afterward, Kit and Angie had come to live with Aunt Velma, their father's sister, in the small house on Rock Garden Lane. Angie had been two, and she remembered little.

But Kit had been eight. Her memories were shaped and lasting. Angie wished she could have a grief equal to Kit's. For her, though, the man and woman existed only as photographs in the heavy metal frames.

Kit pulled out the drawer. From her briefcase

she removed five cartridges for the shotgun she carried in the patrol car. Carefully she put them away.

With equal care, she folded the ten-pound gun belt with its holster, gun, and two pouches of ammunition. The black patent leather gleamed in a ray of evening sunlight.

Angie sat stiffly. The handgun fascinated her. It was a .38, fast-loading, six-shot pistol with a dark wood panel inlaid on each side of the handle.

Now it rested snugly in the holster. Yet its deadliness worked eerily on Angie's mind. The gun seemed much larger than its actual size. She was amazed when it disappeared into the dresser drawer so easily.

Kit turned the lock and dropped the key into her trouser pocket. "Aunt Velma wants to eat out. Any ideas?"

"You choose."

"I could go for Italian."

"Me, too," Angie said, hopping off the bed.

Kit remained by the dresser. "Angie," she said quietly. "About the Wolfpack . . ."

Angie stopped in her tracks.

"No sign of them," Kit said. "They've been quiet since school let out three weeks ago."

"You don't think they've quit?" Angie said anxiously.

"It may be that they've all gone out of town for the summer."

On the drive to the restaurant, Angie struggled with that discouraging possibility. If the Wolfpack had disbanded — if only for the summer — she was wasting time. Jogging for three months might make her the healthiest girl in Dadesville, but it wouldn't solve the break-ins. What, then, was the sense in continuing? So she could start eighth grade with the lowest blood pressure and the darkest suntan in school? Her spirits drooped.

Great Caesar's Restaurant was half empty when they arrived. They chose a table away from the kitchen. Aunt Velma had the cannelloni. Kit ordered spaghetti with white clam sauce, and Angie ordered the same.

"Was it a busy day?" Angie inquired, after the waitress had brought them water.

"Slow," Kit replied. "Five traffic violations, a family dispute, and an injured woman."

"Who is she?" asked Aunt Velma.

"Her name is Clara Blanchard," Kit said. "She's fifty-two and a widow. She's lived in her house three years, alone. According to the neighbors, she keeps to herself and doesn't see anyone except her sister. They go out together a couple of times a week."

"What happend to her?" Angie asked.

"The delivery man from the dry cleaner's stopped by this morning shortly after—eleven o'clock," Kit answered. "He found the door ajar. Mrs. Blanchard lay in the kitchen, bound and

14

gagged. She had been beaten up. The house was ransacked."

"Oh, dear," Aunt Velma said. "Is she badly hurt?"

"She's in the hospital," Kit said. "The doctor won't allow anyone to question her for a day or so."

"You don't know who beat her?" Angie asked.

"That's for the detectives to find out," Kit answered. "I was merely the lead officer."

"Then the person who beat her got away," said Aunt Velma. "How awful."

"Was anything stolen?" asked Angie.

"Perhaps, but we'll have to wait until Mrs. Blanchard can go home and check over her belongings."

"What about clues?" asked Angie.

"The clues don't tell us much," said Kit. "Mrs. Blanchard was doing some cleaning when she was interrupted by the intruder."

"How do you know?" Angie inquired.

"The stove was half cleaned," answered Kit. "There were two cheap, silver-plated candlesticks on the sink counter, and only one had been polished."

Angie sat back. "Where does Mrs. Blanchard live?" she said.

"At two thirty-eight Sixty-third Street," replied Kit.

An idea wriggled into Angie's grasp.

"That's only five blocks from where I was this morning!" she exclaimed.

15

"So?" muttered Kit.

"Don't you see?" Angie said. "He wasn't a salesman!"

"Who?" said Kit and Aunt Velma in unison.

"The man in the tan suit," replied Angie.

"Angie Zane, whatever are you chattering about?" demanded Aunt Velma.

"The man who beat Mrs. Blanchard and probably robbed her," said Angie.

Aunt Velma and Kit regarded her patiently.

Quickly Angie told them about sitting with Jess Berg on his stoop that morning when the blue car stopped on Sixty-eighth Street.

"A man in a tan suit got out," Angie said. "He walked down the street toward us carrying a suitcase. He pretended to ring doorbells."

"How do you know he was pretending?" Kit asked.

"Because nobody answered the bell until he got to the Caseys' house," answered Angie. "It was the only bell he *really* rang."

"Perhaps no one was at home in the other houses," Aunt Velma suggested.

"No," said Angie. Her mind was racing now. It felt thinking-hot, as if she were clicking through a tough exam at school and not just burning imagination.

"At one house," she said, "I saw a woman in an orange housecoat on the second floor. She didn't look out to see who was at the door. And she didn't go downstairs to open it — because the bell hadn't been rung."

"Well," said Aunt Velma in a puzzled voice, "what *was* the man doing?"

"He meant to rob the Caseys' house," Angie said. "Only Mr. Casey, an Air Force sergeant, was home, when normally he would be at the Homestead Air Force Base on Tuesday."

"What was the point of bothering with the other houses?" Kit said. "Why didn't the man go directly to the Caseys'?"

"He tried to throw Jess and me off," said Angie. "He must have spotted us when he drove onto the block. So he stopped immediately, at the far end, and tried to make us think the Caseys' house wasn't special. When he drove off, he did a U-turn to keep us from seeing his license plate."

"Tell me," Kit said. "What connects him with Mrs. Blanchard?"

"The suitcase," Angie replied, "along with Mrs. Blanchard's half-cleaned stove and *one* polished candlestick."

Suddenly Kit seemed genuinely interested. "Go on," she said.

"The man in the tan suit posed as a salesman," continued Angie. "He must be a slick talker, because Mrs. Blanchard let him inside."

"Agreed," Kit said. "Her sister told me she seldom admits visitors and never wants any."

"In the suitcase," Angie said, "the man carried

17

sample cans of *cleaning fluids*. He gave Mrs. Blanchard a demonstration. He cleaned half the stove and one candlestick. When he saw his chance, he knocked her down, tied her up, and went through the house for valuables."

Kit looked amazed, but unconvinced.

"If your theory is right, the man must have scouted the neighborhood beforehand," she said. "He expected Mrs. Blanchard and Mrs. Casey to be alone in their houses on a Tuesday morning."

"But Mrs. Casey wasn't," Angie said, "because her husband, Sergeant Casey, didn't return to the Air Force base Monday. He was home. I saw him speak to the man in the tan suit. The man must have driven directly from the Caseys' to Mrs. Blanchard's.

"Sounds good, but it's all pretty thin," Kit said. "Besides, the man in the tan suit got away."

"Not altogether," Angie said. "I have his license plate number and the description of his car."

"Good going," Kit said. She wrote the information on a paper napkin and immediately left the table to telephone the station.

Aunt Velma had laid down her fork and was sitting perfectly still. She regarded Angie with a mixture of pride and concern.

"You practically solved the case," she said. "But the man in the tan suit must have got a good look at you."

Angie had thought of that. She forced a grin. "I'm not in any danger," she said stoutly.

18

# Chapter
# 3

In the morning Angie biked over to Jess Berg's house. Wheels were a bribe. Jess had refused to help her find the Wolfpack if they jogged.

"Sitting quietly is the secret of good health," he had said. "Keeps the poisons from circulating in your body."

He was waiting with his binoculars and bike. Angie settled beside him on the stoop. She unfolded a map of Dadesville.

"Here's the search area for this morning," she said, tapping Seaward Island.

The sliver of land was about three miles long and less than a half mile wide. Sixteen streets crossed its width. Three streets — Eastshore Drive, Center Street, and Ocean Front Boulevard — ran its length.

"The Wolfpack has hit every part of Dadesville

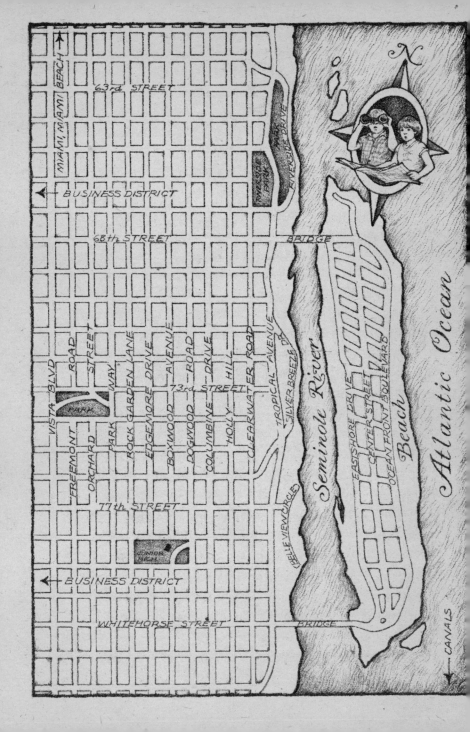

but Seaward Island," Angie said. "It's the natural place for them to strike."

"They'd be crazy to try," Jess said. "With the Sixty-eighth Street Bridge closed, they'd have to use the Whitehorse bridge coming and leaving. It'd be hard for them to escape."

"It won't bother them," Angie insisted. "And there are no stores, just homes. Hardly anyone will be on the streets."

"How about police?" Jess said. "A lot of rich families live on the island. They must demand plenty of police protection. The Wolfpack is too smart to go into a patroled area."

"I asked Kit about that," Angie said. "She told me the police can't give the island all the protection the homeowners want. There aren't enough officers. So a patrol swings through there only at night and on weekends, when the beaches are crowded."

Angie was impatient to get going. But Jess wasn't ready to give in.

"Those rich people have live-in servants," he pointed out. "Burglars steer clear of houses with servants."

"Only the houses along the river and ocean are big and fancy," Angie reminded him. "The houses in the middle of the island, those on Center Street, are much smaller."

Jess sighed. "It's too soon after breakfast to argue. We might as well get on with it."

They pedaled side by side toward the Whitehorse Bridge. *It's better than hunting alone*, Angie thought. *Jess is good company. Besides, he's cute, even if he is overweight and his shirts strain at the buttons.*

As they rode, Jess talked of the joys of bird-watching. He did not mention the Wolfpack until they had passed over the Whitehorse Bridge and were on Seaward Island.

Then he put the question bluntly. "Why spend the summer chasing after those teen-age crooks?" he said. "Is it some kind of crusade with you?"

Angie did not answer immediately. Being at the top of the class hadn't turned Jess's head, and yesterday she had learned he was gentle and considerate.

Still, he might think her reason ridiculous: Finding the Wolfpack would be a small way of thanking Kit for the years of love and support. Jess might burst out laughing and call her sentimental and silly when he heard *that*.

She darted a glance at him. *Husky, not fat*, she thought, and decided to take a chance. She told him what she had not told anyone. "I want to find the Wolfpack for Kit," she said. "When I know who they are, I'll tell Kit. She'll capture them and make sergeant for sure."

Jess didn't laugh. Being Jess, though, he had to examine every side of the subject.

"Aren't you rushing things?" he said. "Kit graduated from the police academy only last March."

"After a year, an officer can take the test for sergeant," Angie told him. "But a high score isn't enough. A good service report is important, too."

Jess said, "Bust the Wolfpack, and Kit won't have to worry about sergeant. She'll jump clear to lieutenant."

Jess meant well, but he couldn't possibly know how much she owed Kit, or how rare in Kit's life was a stroke of good fortune. Kit had worked for everything. Their parents had left so little. Ever since Angie could recall, Kit had held jobs after school — as a bag girl in a supermarket, as a sales girl in Byron's Department Store, as an assistant playground instructor. Aunt Velma's salary at the library was barely enough for one.

There had been boyfriends, but none was able to compete with Kit's schedule. One patient boy, Ted Devlin, the class vice-president, had dated her several times. Angie remembered how Aunt Velma had fussed with Kit's short blond hair whenever the doorbell rang. But after a few months of Sunday afternoon dates, even Ted had stopped calling.

Sacrificing a social life and a college education had not embittered Kit. She never seemed to feel sorry for herself, or resentful. She enjoyed her work and often told Angie that when the right man came along, she would make the time to date him. Still, Angie worried about Kit and wanted to help her.

Jess turned onto Center Street. Angie had to pedal hard to catch up.

The only cars in sight were those parked in driveways. The sky was cloudless, and in the brilliant, scorching light of the sun the cars and trees and houses looked two-dimensional.

The houses on the left stood back to back with the large homes overlooking Eastshore Drive, the Seminole River, and the Dadesville mainland. On the right, the houses backed against the even larger homes facing Ocean Front Boulevard, with the beach and the Atlantic Ocean beyond.

The neighborhood was sleepy. Occasionally Angie heard a television being played too loudly, or the squeals of toddlers splashing in a backyard pool.

Jess created the most activity. Every hundred yards or so he stopped to peer through his binoculars. "A chipping sparrow," he announced, or "A wood thrush. You don't see many here in Florida." And on a small pad he carefully noted every sighting.

They had traveled nearly the length of the island when Jess used the binoculars for the last time that day. "Well, well," he exclaimed, lowering the glasses from his eyes and then lifting them again. "What have we here . . . some new breed of bird?"

His frequent stops to bird-watch had held them up and raised Angie's temperature. She was about to flare at him when she noticed the binoculars. Jess had them aimed down the street at house level.

"What is it?" she asked.

"You might call it a yellow-breasted creeper about to become a road runner," answered Jess. "At the moment, it's perching in a garage window."

"Let me see!" Angie pleaded.

Jess passed her the binoculars. "Next to the last house on the right."

The angle and the glasses enabled Angie to see past a row of palms. She spied a boy in a yellow shirt and blue jeans disappearing into a garage window.

"I've seen him before," she gasped. "He's a ninth grader. His name is —"

"Frank Congdon," supplied Jess, "and that's not his garage. He lives across the street."

"The Wolfpack!" Angie cried.

Jess didn't seem to hear.

"The Wolfpack!" Angie repeated. "We've found them!"

"Keep your voice down," said Jess. "Don't disturb me when I'm shaking."

"Let's move in before they get away," Angie urged.

"You move in," Jess encouraged her. "I'll stay here."

"Quit clowning," Angie said. "We'll simply observe them. We'll make believe we're out for a nature ride."

"Show biz," mumbled Jess.

They pedaled at a slow, nature-ride pace.

"No one will ever take us for serious students of crime," Angie said confidently. "We'll look like two innocent bird-watchers from Venus."

"You don't think we found the Wolfpack, do you?" Angie accused.

"Nope," said Jess. "If I did, I'd be heading the other way."

"Suppose it *is* the Wolfpack," Angie said. "Will you run?"

Jess reflected upon the question. "I'll do what the cops do on television," he replied. "First I'll holler, 'Freeze!' Then I'll run."

"How do you know the rest of the gang isn't hiding in the house?"

"I'll find out," said Jess. "I'll shout, 'Olly, olly oxen free.'"

"You shout that at the end of hide-and-seek."

"Well, doesn't everyone come out of hiding?"

"Grrr," said Angie.

As they drew even with the garage, Jess became serious. "Stay here," he said. "I'll have a look around the corner."

He could be maddeningly silly, Angie decided, but when he wasn't fooling around, his steadiness was a comfort. She watched him round the corner and return a few seconds later.

"All clear," he reported. "Not a teenager or a truck in sight. Frank Congdon has to be a loner."

They left their bikes by a fire hydrant and slipped behind the row of palms that shielded the side of the garage from the street. The window was still open.

"I can hear him inside," Angie whispered.

They ducked past the window and posted themselves at the rear of the garage, out of sight.

The window squeaked. Angie stiffened and nudged Jess.

The next moment she heard the dull thud of Frank dropping to the ground.

"Hi, Frank," Jess called, without revealing himself.

"W-who's there?" came the frightened reply.

Jess and Angie stepped into view.

Frank was poised in a half crouch. He held a fistful of ball-point pens. He glanced around quickly, eyes worried and narrowed. Satisfied that he had merely two children to deal with, he straightened and put on a threatening front.

"You don't belong here," he snarled.

"Neither do you," Jess answered. He strolled past Frank and stopped at the row of palms, blocking Frank's escape across the street to his house.

Angie was left to guard the passage into the backyard. All at once her legs felt like marmalade.

"Put the pens back," Jess said.

"You're spoiling for it," Frank jeered. "Get out of my way."

"First the pens."

Angie was scared. She hadn't imagined her spying would lead to a fight, maybe with someone getting hurt.

"Well?" Jess said. He was heavier than Frank, but shorter and a year younger.

Frank glared. "Nuts to you, fat boy," he growled, and charged.

He swung at Jess's face with the pens. Angie couldn't be sure of the rest, except that Jess ducked and the punch missed. Then Jess's fists were hammering Frank's stomach.

Very shortly, Frank's legs quivered and he let out a wail of surrender. Immediately Jess lowered his hands.

The older boy sagged to the ground. He came to rest on his side, his legs curled up, his face contorted with pain and shock.

The one-sided fight was over. Angie gaped in disbelief. Frank hadn't landed a blow. He was down and laboring for breath. Jess was unmarked.

She looked from Frank to Jess and back to Frank. She was torn between concern for Frank and admiration for Jess.

"He'll be all right," Jess assured her. "I knocked the wind out of him. His ribs will be sore for a couple of days."

Frank's body wrenched for air, and he wheezed like a rusty flute.

"My father taught me," explained Jess, "in a bare-handed fight, you never shoot for the head. You can break your knuckles."

"You must have broken my ribs," panted Frank. "Why'd you do that?"

"I had an idea you were trying to run off with some pens," replied Jess.

Frank struggled off the ground. He stood doubled over and swaying.

"Find a doctor," he moaned. "Take me to the hospital. Tell 'em I fell off the roof. Oooh . . ."

"You big faker," Angie said. "You can talk."

"Huh?"

"Talk," Jess said. "You've heard the word, I'm sure. You don't have to write away for details."

"What's all the fuss about?" whined Frank. "I swiped eight cheap pens. Big deal. Don't tell me you never snitched anything."

Angie didn't answer. Jess wigwagged a fist.

"Okay, okay!" yelped Frank. He couldn't take another of Jess's body treatments.

For more than a year, he said, he'd been taking a shortcut to the beach past the garage. Six months ago he had noticed that the window, which had frosted glass, was open. He had peeked in.

"I didn't think about stealing," he said. "But the garage is like a treasure chest. It's got stacks of electric light bulbs, paper napkins, bars of soap, and other stuff. You name it."

Angie went to the window and peeped. "So far," she said, "you're telling the truth."

"The next day the window was closed," Frank continued. "I figured a way to jimmy it. I've been helping myself ever since."

"Who lives here?" asked Jess.

"Mr. Wells," Frank answered. "He owns the convenience store on Hibiscus and Pine View."

"Golly, I know him," Angie said. "He's neat. I've seen him sell candy to kids who are a penny or two short. Why steal from *him?*"

"It's so easy," Frank said with a shrug. "It's kind of like a hobby. Heck, nothing in the whole garage is worth more than a buck or two."

"Mr. Wells probably uses the garage as a stockroom for some of the goods he sells at his store," Jess said. "He must not have enough storage space there. If he catches you, he'll have you arrested."

"No chance," asserted Frank slyly. "Mr. Wells goes away for a few days every month. On buying trips, I guess. I don't go near this place when he's home."

"Does he live alone?" asked Angie, feeling very much the full-fledged detective. "I've heard him talk about his son."

"After his wife died, his widowed sister came to keep house for him," Frank said. "But she moved out three years ago. A month later, his son got a job up in New York. Since then Mr. Wells has lived alone."

Angie was vaguely reminded of something, but the thought vanished before she could snag it. Jess was speaking.

"I suggest you put back the pens," he said sternly. "And if you have an ounce of brains, you'll use another shortcut to the beach."

"Hey, you're not going to tell on me?" Frank said.

"We won't tell," Angie said, "if you promise to quit stealing."

"Never again. I'll take the long way to the beach, I promise!" Frank jabbered.

He returned the pens, closed the window, and pulled his pockets inside out to prove his newfound honesty.

"Scoot," Jess said.

Frank required no urging. He bolted.

Angie sighed. "Another child saved from a life of crime."

"Until Mr. Wells leaves on his next trip," Jess said.

They biked down the last three blocks of Center Street. One car drove by, a station wagon loaded with children.

At the Sixty-eighth Street Bridge they watched the construction for a while. Then they rode back along Eastshore Drive toward the Whitehorse Bridge.

They spoke little. Angie wondered if they had handled Frank Congdon wisely.

"See you tomorrow," Jess said as they stopped at his house.

"Same time," Angie replied. "We'll catch the Wolfpack." She spoke forcefully, with more confidence than she felt.

Her hunch had told her the Wolfpack would hit

Seaward Island today. Yet all they had caught was a boy swiping some ball-point pens.

*Don't give up,* she thought stubbornly. She pushed off and pedaled home, her determination to keep up the hunt as strong as ever.

There was something else . . . something in the back of her mind. But she didn't know what it was.

# Chapter
# 4

Kit seldom brought home the concerns of her job, but she was solemnly quiet when she arrived that evening. She greeted Angie and Aunt Velma with her usual warmth and then went directly to her room.

Angie held her tongue, though she was dying to talk about Frank Congdon and the fight with Jess. She sensed that what was troubling Kit was more important.

Not until they were seated at dinner did Kit reveal what was on her mind. "Can you describe the mystery man you saw yesterday?" she began. "The one in the tan suit."

"He was tall — I guess over six feet — well built and dark-haired," Angie said. "He carried a suitcase."

"Mrs. Blanchard talked to Lieutenant Evans

this afternoon in the hospital," Kit said. "The man who attacked her in her house pretended to be from the Power and Light Company."

"Does he fit my description?" Angie asked anxiously.

Kit shook her head. "Mrs. Blanchard says the man was short, fat, blond, and wore a green uniform. We'll have a more complete picture of what he was after when Mrs. Blanchard goes home tomorrow. She'll know then what was stolen."

"You mean the man in the tan suit had nothing to do with Mrs. Blanchard?" asked Aunt Velma, who had taken the news almost as hard as Angie.

"Nothing at all," Kit said, speaking softly to ease their disappointment.

But her next words couldn't be softened. "The Wolfpack struck today," she said. "On Seaward Island."

Angie started in surprise. How was it possible? Jess and she were there this morning!

Kit proceeded to recount the facts. The house that had been robbed belonged to the Weygand family, who were spending the summer in Europe. Their maid had gone shopping at nine o'clock, leaving the house empty for more than two hours.

Upon her return, the maid discovered that a rear window had been forced. Three television sets, a videotape recording machine, and all the expensive jewelry Mrs. Weygand had left behind were missing.

The lone witness was an elderly man who had been walking the beach looking for shells. He had noticed a yellow van drive up to the Weygands' front door, as if making a delivery. Since nothing seemed peculiar, he hadn't bothered to watch.

"It was the Wolfpack," Kit said emphatically. "As usual, they called the station and bragged about the robbery."

During the rest of the meal, Angie scarcely touched her food. She sat silently, wanting to ask a million questions and yet not wanting to betray her sense of failure. She had missed the golden opportunity to spot the Wolfpack. A second chance might never come.

As Kit and Aunt Velma chatted, she sagged lower and lower in her chair. Their voices sounded far away. Aunt Velma, who worked at the South Branch Library, talked about the new summer reading program for children. Kit reviewed her day, one of traffic violations and family squabbles.

Angie excused herself early and trudged to her room. She fell onto the bed fully clothed and lay unmoving, pressed down by helplessness and the burden of being too young.

Frank Congdon, darn him! If only he hadn't chosen this morning to rob Mr. Wells. While she and Jess worried over a few ball-point pens, the Wolfpack had been at work.

She knew one thing. The yellow van would not have fooled her. She'd have taken down the license plate number. And she'd have got a good look at the gang. Then she'd have picked them out from the photos in an old high-school yearbook.

As night fell, Kit knocked and entered the room noiselessly. She sat down at the foot of the bed.

"Are you going to give up on the Wolfpack?" she asked.

"Is there any point in going on?"

"Seaward Island stretches nearly three miles," said Kit. "No one can possibly keep an eye on what's happening there every minute."

Angie rolled toward the wall. She hated herself for turning away, but she hated herself more for being a bumbler. She could not face kindness right then.

"I got into police work because I want to help people," Kit said, "and I like being around officers who feel the same way. Maybe if I'd gone to college I'd be helping as a doctor or a lawyer. But I'm not unhappy with what I'm doing. You really don't have to make it better."

She laid her hand lightly on Angie's ankle.

"Of course, some of the job is boring, and I do my share of clock-watching," she continued. "And much of it is an exercise in patience. I'll tell you something. I've been trying to catch a ring of counterfeiters ever since I put on a uniform. A few of the phony bills, twenties, have been passed right here in town."

"You're a police officer," Angie said dully. "You

know what to do. You're trained."

"Yesterday," said Kit, "two of the bills were passed in area two, my area this month. Right under my nose. I have to be patient. I have to wait. I'll follow leads and keep chugging till I find the counterfeiters."

Angie twisted around. After a few seconds she asked, "Do you really think I should go on?"

"Yes, but not for me — for yourself," Kit said. "Give up on the Wolfpack, and you'll start giving up on everything."

Angie bounced up to a sitting position. "What is the address of the Weygand house?"

A trace of a smile played on the corners of Kit's lips. "Five three five one Ocean Front Boulevard. I'll write it down."

She crossed to Angie's desk and scribbled on a piece of paper. Then she kissed Angie on the forehead. "Good night, sis."

"Good night," Angie responded. They grinned at each other.

Angie lay awake for what seemed hours, thinking. Then she finally fell asleep. The morning sun awakened her. It was nearly eight o'clock.

After breakfast, she telephoned Jess and told him about the Wolfpack. "Let's ride out to the Weygand house and have a look around," she suggested. "We may find some clues."

"Can't," said Jess. "Something's come up. I'm going to visit my grandmother in Miami Beach."

Miami Beach was seventy miles away. Jess would be gone the entire day.

"I'll poke around by myself," Angie said. "Maybe I can get to talk with the maid."

"Good luck," said Jess, and added, "Watch your nose."

Angie gave her bed a lick and a promise, tucking in only the side that showed. She surveyed the room: Yesterday's clothes lay where she had discarded them — all over. She scooped everything into a wad and whizzed it under the bed with a well-drilled hand. A couple of hook kicks sent a stray sock after the other garments, and the room was in order.

She was at the front door before she remembered that Kit had written the Weygands' address on a sheet of paper that lay on her desk. The words *Ocean Front Boulevard* were clear enough. But the house number before the words was either 5351 or 5357. Kit had written rapidly in the darkness and had scrawled the last digit. It could be either a one or a seven.

Which was it? Angie couldn't be positive. But suddenly the need to decide vanished. An idea, cloudy but nagging, stirred in her mind.

After a bit she realized what it was. She'd been wrong about the man in the tan suit. He hadn't intended to rob the *Caseys'* house. . . .

"Wow!" she cried, and set off at a spirited jog for Sixty-eighth Street and Jess's house. He had already left when she arrived. Well, she'd simply have to do it herself. She sat down on the stoop and gazed at the Casey house, screwing up her courage.

"Get going, you 'fraidy cat," she admonished herself.

She rose and slanted across the street. She was right. The number above the Caseys' door was 238. So far, so good.

A woman answered the doorbell. "What is it?" She was young and friendly.

"My name is Angie Zane," Angie said politely. "I'm here to speak with Sergeant Casey."

"Bill won't be home till Friday night," the woman replied. "He lives on the base weekdays. Can I help you? I'm Mrs. Casey."

"I'd like to ask you about the man in the tan suit who came to your house two days ago. In the morning. A salesman. At least, he carried a suitcase."

"Why, yes, there was a man," replied Mrs. Casey. "Bill spoke to him. But he wasn't a salesman, at least not a good one."

"What do you mean?"

"He didn't even try to sell Bill anything," Mrs. Casey replied. "He just stood there looking astonished."

"He wasn't selling household cleaner?"

"No, all he did was apologize for disturbing us," said Mrs. Casey. "Bill felt sorry for him. He said the poor man would starve to death in a week if he didn't find some other line of work."

"Thank you," said Angie. "Thank you very much!"

Giddy with excitement, she walked half a block on feet that fairly sprang from the pavement. Then, unable to hold back, she broke into a lope.

Hunting the Wolfpack had thrown her headlong into another mystery, and she set her teeth into it. In no time she had covered five blocks. She cut south onto Sixty-third Street and halted. Most of the houses were without numbers out front. She had to ask two girls who were playing hopscotch on the sidewalk which one was Mrs. Blanchard's house.

"Over there," answered one of the girls, waving a dirty hand toward a two-story gray house with black shutters.

"You'd better stay away from Mrs. Blanchard," said the second girl. "She'll cast a spell over you, and you'll wind up as a geranium or a sunflower."

"Ethel, sssh!" said the first girl.

"Don't *sssh* me, Patsy," Ethel said. "Mrs. Blanchard turns children into flowers and sticks them in those pots."

On the ledge outside a second-floor window were two large earthenware pots filled with geraniums.

"Don't go near her," Ethel warned. "She's a witch."

"Ethel, shut up!" cried Patsy.

"She's a witch and you know it," Ethel retorted.

"Nonsense," objected Angie. "Lots of people keep flowers on windowsills. My Aunt Velma has gladiolus this time of year."

"But she waters them," declared Ethel. "Mrs. Blanchard never waters her flowers. She *replaces* them."

Now that the horrible black secret was out, Patsy shrugged resignedly and joined in. "Nobody knows how many children have fallen into her clutches," she said gravely. "The police list them as runaways. The facts would spread panic."

"She hardly ever goes out during the day," put in Ethel, attempting a leer. "She hides inside and stirs her cauldron."

"You ought to find something better to do than make up wicked stories about Mrs. Blanchard," Angie said. "It isn't funny, The poor woman was beaten and her house turned inside out."

"Not on your life," snorted Ethel. "Her cauldron blew up and wrecked everything."

Angie mastered her temper. *Boy, are you ever crazy*, she thought. She said only, "I've got to be going." She walked away, leaving the pair to their hopscotch and their weird make-believe.

"Look out," Ethel called, "or she'll plant you at midnight."

"Upside down in a mustard jar," chimed in Patsy.

They continued to chant impish horrors. Angie

paid them no mind. She had seen the number nailed above Mrs. Blanchard's door. It was partly hidden by the fronds of a palm tree, but it was very much the right number — 238.

Angie sidled a few steps to her right until she could see into the backyard. Trimmed hedges bordered a winding stone path that led from a patio through a garden of tropical foliage. Here and there sprouted patches of geraniums and sunflowers.

Suddenly an uncomfortable feeling, like a cold breath, ran up her spine. She thought she was being watched . . .

She glanced guardedly at the house. The windows stared back blankly. She swung around. Patsy and Ethel were across the street, quarreling like alley cats.

A movement farther down the block pricked her curiosity. A car pulled from the curb and crept in her direction.

Angie couldn't see the dented right fender that Jess had spied through his binoculars. She recognized the car nonetheless.

It was the same blue, five-year-old Chevy two-door. Angie could not make him out, but she had no doubt about who was behind the wheel — the man in the tan suit.

# Chapter
# 5

The sight of the blue car shocked Angie. Her legs went spongy, and she had to suck in breath. She moved away from Mrs. Blanchard's house and walked as fast as she could without appearing to flee. *Stay cool*, she thought. *Don't look back*.

She and the man in the tan suit were on the same street for the second time in two days. A harmless coincidence? "He isn't a salesman. He was just looking for a place to stay. He rented a room from Mrs. Blanchard and lives here now," she lied to herself. The explanation served her head, for it sounded reasonable. It failed, however, to quiet the pounding of her heart.

At the first corner she decided to test him, to find out for sure if he was following her. Instead of

44

continuing straight on, she turned south and broke into a trot.

The neighborhood was one through which she had jogged before. The houses were small, and the cars in the driveways looked old and thirsting for paint. The people seemed friendly. Surely they would help in an emergency.

Conquering the urge to sprint all out, she found her pace and settled into it. The idea of zigzagging through backyards occurred to her. She discarded the idea. She had to know if he was after her.

"It's your hot little imagination again," she reproached herself. "He lives on Sixty-third Street and is going off to visit a sick horse."

Sick horse or not, it was sensible to make *sure* of him. The best course was to stick to her pose as a jogger out for a morning three-miler.

*Steady on*, she thought.

As she ran, the tension gradually drained from her legs. Her muscles relaxed, and her breathing became normal. Her heart ceased to pound like a clanging kettle.

She jogged six blocks before drawing up at the Morgan Boulevard traffic light. An elderly woman waiting by the curb eyed her red-and-white running shoes.

"Do you run every day?" she inquired.

"If the weather permits," Angie answered.

"I don't think it's good for young girls," the woman said.

"Some days it comes in handy," Angie remarked dryly.

The woman shrugged. Then she shrugged again.

The traffic light was still against her. Casually, as if watching a flight of birds, Angie shifted sideways and glanced back.

The blue car was there.

She recalled crossing Morgan Boulevard. After that, her mind switched off against the onrush of fear. The next half mile was a blank.

The sidewalk ended. Her feet hit the rough earth, jarringly. She recovered her bearings.

The Dadesville town limit lay a short distance ahead. The number of homes around her had dwindled. They were older and farther apart now. Another quarter mile, and the land would level into undeveloped stretches of pine and saw palmetto. The buildings were few there, and the roads lonely.

*I'm heading just where it will be easy for him!* she thought. Her mouth was dry with the taste of rubber bands. She stopped while she still felt somewhat protected by homes and people nearby, and cars moving along the street.

Was he following?

She pulled out her handkerchief. The pennies spilled free. She knelt and looked.

The blue car was angled into the curb. Her unexpected stop had caught its driver by surprise, leaving him no time to park properly. The front end was tucked behind a brown sports car. The rear stuck out like a gleaming flank. The car was no longer a machine to Angie. It resembled a stalking animal, hiding and waiting.

At least now she was positive. He *was* following her.

To ring a doorbell and beg help would only call attention to herself. She had to get away without putting him wise. If she could give him the slip, he'd never know who she was or where to find her.

The business district downtown . . . she could lose herself quite naturally among the shoppers and cars and stores.

She mopped her face with the handkerchief and picked up the pennies. To leave them behind would be a tip-off. Her fingers were stiff and shaking, and it took her a frightfully long time to gather all ten.

"Now, go!"

She ran, deliberately holding back her speed to match her earlier pace. In fifteen minutes she had reached the busy intersection of Hibiscus and Main. She slumped against a parked car, weary and weak with relief.

A young coupled passed. The man grinned at her panting figure. "Next year the Boston Marathon, eh, kid?" he cracked.

Angie thought, *Boston would be a snap.*

When she'd regained her wind, she walked a

block up Hibiscus — a one-way street where the blue car could not follow — to Pine View. She passed Bartlett's Shoe Store and the barber shop. Reaching Mr. Well's convenience store on the corner, she flattened herself against the tile wall, inched forward, and peeked around.

She saw him instantly. He had left the car and was walking with light, athletic steps in her direction. He wore a checkered gray sports jacket and charcoal trousers, but it was he.

Without thinking twice, she took refuge in the convenience store. It was empty except for two plump women customers, poring over the bakery goods.

The cash register was manned by Jenny Wise, a college student who clerked part-time. Jenny was a friend of Kit's. All the same, Angie wished Mr. Wells were there. He was a large, easygoing man who liked children. Nonetheless, Angie felt he could be mean if he had to be, mean enough to handle the man outside.

But Mr. Wells wasn't there to offer protection. Angie loafed along the first aisle, feigning interest in the hair dyes, lipsticks, and other boxed, do-it-yourself miracles for instant beauty and popularity. Halfway down the aisle she lifted her gaze. The front window allowed her to see across the street. He was there, tilting his head as he pulled a match to a cigarette with cupped hands.

He wouldn't dare do anything to her in the presence of three witnesses. For the time being she was safe. On the other hand, she couldn't hide in the store all day.

Except for the entrance, the only door was in the rear. On it was fixed a narrow metal sign with curved ends: "Keep Out."

Angie strolled to the checkout counter. "Could I possibly use your washroom? It's an emergency."

"Mr. Wells doesn't like anyone in the back but employees," Jenny Wise said. She hesitated. "Oh, I guess it's all right in your case. Through the rear door and just to the left."

"Thanks," said Angie. Her feet were already in motion.

The door led to a large storeroom filled with rows of freestanding shelves. Because the shelves were almost bare, she had no trouble spying at the far end exactly what she sought — an exit.

Without wasting a second, she plunged outside. Bright sunlight burned her eyes. Squinting, she stumbled once, saved her balance, and ran with every ounce of her strength.

Two hours later she was in her room, having run a mini-marathon through the streets of Dadesville, circling, retracing her steps, checking and double-checking. She had escaped him. Of that she was satisfied. Nevertheless, she went to the window and looked up and down the street. Neither the blue car nor the mystery man was to be seen.

The strain of the day hit Angie full force. The

nervous energy on which she had been living was used up. She fell on her bed, sobbing with fright and exhaustion.

Presently she drifted into a shallow, restless sleep and awoke a little before six o'clock. She showered and changed clothes. Brushing her hair, she wondered: *How am I going to tell Aunt Velma and Kit?*

The opportunity came midway through dinner. Angie had spoken little, waiting tensely for the right opening. Kit introduced the subject. "Mrs. Blanchard reported what was stolen from her," she said. "Cash and jewelry."

"I don't understand why that man had to beat her," Aunt Velma said.

"When she refused to tell him where she hid her valuables, I suppose he lost his head," Kit said.

Now was the moment. "Did you ever check the license plate of the blue car I told you about?" Angie asked.

"No," said Kit. "Your man in the tan suit didn't fit the description of the robber, remember?"

Angie said offhandedly, "I saw the blue car again today."

"Where?"

"In town," said Angie. "This morning. The man got out of the car and walked toward me. I think he recognized me."

"And?"

Angie snipped the story short. She wouldn't be

permitted out of the house if she told how far she'd been followed.

"I ran into Mr. Wells's store," she said.

"He followed you?" Kit said.

"He stopped outside."

"Kit," said Aunt Velma. The line on her brow had deepened. "It wouldn't hurt to run his license number through Central's computer and find out who he is."

"I can't do that without cause," Kit replied.

"Did he speak to you, Angie?" Aunt Velma asked.

"No, he just waited outside the store and lit a cigarette."

Kit leaned forward. "How long did he wait?"

"I don't know," Angie said. "I sneaked out the back." Her self-control, so shakily held together all day, was crumbling under the impact of reliving the morning. "I ran."

"You really think he was following you?" Kit said. "Really?"

"Yes," said Angie, her eyes moist. "He scared me."

Kit looked at her steadily.

"That's cause," she said.

Throughout the next day, Angie stayed in the house with the doors locked. She ventured out only to fetch the mail. Jess called around noon. They arranged to meet the next morning.

At four o'clock Kit's key clicking in the lock was

the most welcome of sounds. Everything was right again, safe and good, with Kit in the house.

"All quiet?" she asked Angie.

"Yes."

"The street just now was clear," Kit said. "No strangers."

"I gave him the slip. I'm certain I did."

"Well, I have something for you," Kit announced.

She was putting her gun and ammunition into the dresser drawer. She spoke over her shoulder.

"A doctor in Plantation reported a five-year-old Chevy two-door stolen from his office parking lot last week. It was green, but it had dents in the right rear fender. We think it's the same car with different plates and a fast repaint job."

Angie heard, and she worked the piece of information around in her mind. She nudged it until it dropped solidly into place — between the two houses with the same number, 238.

# Chapter
# 6

It was Jess's idea to return to Seaward Island. "The Wolfpack has never struck twice in the same week," he said. "And never twice in a row in the same neighborhood. They're due to change their pattern."

Angie was less than enthusiastic about biking off on such a long shot. Yet doing something was better than sitting home and worrying. "The island is as good a place as any to scout," she agreed halfheartedly.

Arguing would be an error. She wanted to keep Jess in his present mood. When she had told him about being followed yesterday, his happy-go-lucky manner had vanished. His face had hardened. "I'm going to stick close to you all day," he had vowed.

Despite herself, she had tingled pleasantly. The

sensation of having a boy look after her was new. Angie Zane, crime fighter, had blushed.

Of course, Jess's suggestion to search Seaward Island was a dodge. She knew very well that he wanted to take her mind off the mystery man. After robbing the Weygand house on Ocean Front Boulevard, the Wolfpack would lie low for several days. Seaward Island would be the quietest and safest place for them to be.

As they pedaled, Angie shot him a shy glance. He was riding with military alertness, shifting his gaze constantly as he watched for the blue car.

They chatted little, and neither teased each other nor clowned around. Although the stress of being followed was ever-present, the trip passed uneventfully.

After they had crossed the Whitehorse Bridge and were on the island, Jess suggested a walk on the beach.

"Later," Angie said. "When it's past the time for the Wolfpack to strike."

Jess objected, and one word led to another till they were quarreling. Angie wanted Jess to stay by the bridge; from there he could see every vehicle entering or leaving the island.

"I'll ride around for an hour or so," she said.

Jess insisted on accompanying her. "We don't have to bike," he said. "We could walk on the beach and keep an eye on Ocean Front Boulevard. It'll be safer."

"And practically useless," Angie said. Her voice rose royally. "I'm not going to stroll on the sand while there is the slightest chance of spotting the Wolfpack!"

It was the most serious disagreement she had had with Jess. He yielded at last to the stubborn strain of independence in her.

"Don't become a victim," he warned, regarding her with grudging admiration. "Victims don't wear medals."

"If I see a yellow van or a blue car, I'll dazzle you," Angie replied. "I'll put on moves you won't be able to tell from greased lightning."

"You don't mind if I worry a little?" Jess said. He leaned his bike against a pine tree and sat down, resigned.

Angie started down Eastshore Drive alone. At every cross street, she looked to her right toward Center Street and Ocean Front Boulevard. She saw nothing out of the ordinary.

The road stopped at the line of wooden horses fencing off the construction at the Sixty-eighth Street Bridge. She turned east, passed Center Street, and headed back to Jess along Ocean Front Boulevard.

The vast Atlantic floated to her left, and she had a good view of nearly the whole beach. Men, women, and childern dotted the sand and surf.

The air was still. Sleepy wavelets lazed shoreward, foaming and flattening in their endless cycle. The sky shone with the sparkle of blue frost, and the entire scene seemed to have been chipped off a forgotten edge of the world.

About a mile offshore, a dozen pleasure boats had formed a cluster. "Dolphin must be running," Angie thought idly.

She read the address on a big pink house to her right and realized the Weygand house must be three blocks farther. She wondered if she had the spunk to question the maid about the robbery.

*I could have the door slammed in my face,* Angie thought, steeling herself for the worst.

On second thought, the worst might be a lot worse than a squashed nose. Suppose the maid had been secretly in league with the Wolfpack? *She* would put the questions. "Why do you want to know these things, honey? What's your name? Where do you live?"

Angie thought of a good many more questions a guilty, suspicious maid might ask her, and of how she could squirm away. "I'll just say, 'Sorry, I have the wrong house.' " No, that wouldn't fool a gerbil.

The best scheme would be to leave the maid believing she had been the object of a childish prank. "I'll say I'm a poor peasant girl come to pay her taxes," Angie decided, "and light out."

The fancied contest with the maid never came to pass. As Angie reached the midpoint of the island, her attention veered to something else — a boat.

A sport fisherman with a flybridge, it had come barreling from the north. It sped along with bow tilted haughtily, not two hundred yards from the shoreline.

*Too close*, Angie thought.

The boat held to a string-straight course. Out beyond the other swimmers, a woman basked on a rubber raft. She lay facedown, ignorant of her danger.

The boat bore down upon her unheedingly. It swerved not one degree and swept by her with scarcely a yard to spare.

The wake cuffed raft and woman furiously, flipping them over. The woman hurtled high into the air, legs skyward. The raft rose even higher, hung like a kite, and then bounced twice on the surface before jerking about in the churned water.

A man on the beach leaped to his feet and shook his fist. "Crazy fool!" he roared at the boat.

The woman in the water bobbed up. She swam for the raft, apparently unhurt. She threw both her arms over it and held on.

The boat slowed and stopped. Angie could see two men aboard. Up on the flybridge, a man in a blue shirt sat at the controls. Below him on the open rear deck was a man in a red shirt.

Red Shirt started to climb the ladder to the flybridge. When he got halfway up, Blue Shirt left the controls, gripped the top rails of the ladder, and kicked.

Red Shirt hung on. But with two more kicks, Blue Shirt sent him reeling back.

Metal flashed in Red Shirt's hand. As he made for the ladder again, a man in a sleeveless undershirt burst from the cabin. He lunged at Red Shirt.

For a few moments Angie lost sight of the sport fisherman, as traffic screened her field of vision. A white van and two station wagons, going toward the Whitehorse Bridge, drove in front of her.

By the time she awoke to the van, it was fifty feet down the road. A van! The cars behind it blocked most of the license plate, but Angie made out the last number — eight.

*Jess will get it all*, she thought.

She returned her attention to the boat. The two men on deck were still struggling violently. Red Shirt's arm was held above his head by the other man. Then a gunshot sounded.

By now everyone on the beach was watching. Some screamed, and a few stood frozen in disbelief. Most hurried to the water's edge for a closer view.

The two men struggled back and forth. Suddenly Red Shirt wrestled free. A second report cracked across the water. The other man clutched his chest with both hands, staggered back against the ladder, and grabbed it with his left hand for support.

Like a startled sea creature, the boat rammed forward under full throttle and raced off.

A teenager who had been cutting the lawn two houses from Angie shut off his mower. "I better call the Coast Guard," he shouted to no one in particular, and raced into the house.

As the boat disappeared behind a spit of sand, Angie heard another gunshot. Then, as if to prove that what she had seen had really happened, two more shots sounded.

It was not a bad dream. It was a bad dream come true.

Jess was waiting for her where Ocean Front Boulevard curved from the beach. "Did you see it?"

Angie shuddered. "I saw it."

They stood side by side. Numbly they stared at the ocean, now healed of the horror and rolling serenely in the honey-colored sunlight.

Angie said, "The Coast Guard has been called."

"Good," said Jess.

Neither could think of anything more to say.

After a while Angie remembered. "I saw a white van."

"So did I," Jess said. "I didn't pay it much attention. I was running to the beach after the first shot, and I saw it coming down the road toward me, with some cars following."

"The last number of its license plate is eight," said Angie. "That ought to help."

"Dunno," Jess said. "We can't look all over South Florida for a white Chevy van three years old with an eight."

"It was a three-year-old Ford," Angie corrected.

"Chevy."

Jess was good at cars. But he was flat wrong this time.

"Ford," Angie said again. "My Uncle Bert has one just like it."

"Chevy or Ford, what's the difference?" Jess declared. "The Wolfpack has made us van-nutty. Yellow or white, there must be fifty of each in Dadesville alone."

"Ummmh," Angie agreed absently. An idea had rooted in her mind. "We can find that boat."

Jess's eyebrows lifted in surprise. "How?"

"It continued south after the shooting, in the direction of the Coast Guard Station at Hobeson Sound," Angie said. "The men on board must have assumed the Coast Guard was notified."

"So?"

"So any boat answering the description of theirs will be stopped on sight. They have to hide."

"Where?" said Jess. "It's thirteen miles from here to Hobeson Sound."

"They'd duck into one of the canals," Angie said. "There are only six of them along the route deep enough for that boat."

"How do you know?" inquired Jess.

"Sometimes Aunt Velma and I fish the canals on weekends," Angie replied.

"This fish is about fifty feet long," Jess said, an edge of warning in his tone.

He looked at Angie hopefully, but her eyes had darkened with determination.

"All right," he said. "It might be fun just to look."

Riding off Seaward Island, Angie felt her blood draw into a lump of misgivings. She had pounced on this new challenge, and she had convinced Jess to join her. Now they were hurrying toward — what?

She had started the summer with a definite purpose. She had wanted to spot the Wolfpack for Kit. And Kit, meanwhile, was intent on nabbing a band of counterfeiters. But counterfeiters and teenage thieves were minor lawbreakers compared to people who shot people. Now, unintentionally, she was going after real criminals.

"You're lagging," Jess called to her. "C'mon. We've got a lot of ground to cover."

# Chapter
# 7

By two o'clock Angie was thirsty, sweaty, and achy. She had biked, crouched, crawled, crept, torn her shorts, scratched her knees, and banged her shins. Up and down canals she had peered and pored. She had begun to see boats when she looked at billboards.

She and Jess had scouted four canals. The sport fisherman was nowhere to be seen.

Jess ran a handkerchief over his drenched face. His shirt had come untucked and his cutoff jeans sagged, baring a space of perspiration-wet tummy.

"Four down and two to go," he said wearily.

"All the canals are beginning to look alike," Angie confessed. "But we can't quit yet."

The fifth canal was different. The first four were inland waterways of a mile or more, lined by homes that boasted their own docks. The fifth wound for less than a half mile through barren tracts. It ended at a marina that served the mini-mansions of Dadesville Estates.

From one position, Angie and Jess could scan all the boats at a single sweep.

Leaving their bikes, they crept through the undergrowth a hundred yards downstream of the marina. Near the water's edge, Jess knelt on both knees and looked through his binoculars. He moved the glasses slowly from left to right and stopped.

"See it?" queried Angie.

"I see it," Jess whispered, and dropped down on his heels.

"Are you sure?"

"Yep, except the registration numbers on the bow seem funny."

"Then it's not our sport fisherman," said Angie.

Jess handed her the binoculars. "It has to be the same boat," he said. "It had a broken rail on the port side of the flybridge. So does this one."

Angie aimed the binoculars at the flybridge. "Yesss," she murmured. "Yes, yes!"

"Well, we found it," said Jess with satisfaction. "What now?"

"We take a closer look," declared Angie.

"I'd better tune up my ears," Jess said. "I thought you said we should take a closer look."

"We're detectives, aren't we?" snapped Angie.

Jess's round face lengthened. "I'm a coward for

all seasons," he said. Then his chin lifted, and he squeezed out a smile. "Lead on."

The marina was protected by a tall wire fence, but the gate stood open. Between the gate and the yachts was a tiny pink building, the dockmaster's office. To the right was a gas pump and a ramp down which small boats were launched from trailers.

As Angie and Jess entered the enclosure, a droopy-shouldered man in whites came out of the office. He carried a clipboard thick with papers, and trudged as if any effort would bring on an energy crisis.

"You kids from around here?" he asked.

"We are," answered Angie. Dadesville Estates, after all, was in Dadesville and not in Miami or Wyoming.

"Good," grunted the man, and he dismissed them from his concerns.

He read the pump, wrote in his clipboard, and returned to the office with the speed of a glacier. Through the glass panels of the door, Angie saw him sit down at a desk, his back to the sport fisherman.

As with all the boats, the sport fisherman was docked stern first. The name on the transom, *The Blowing Clear*, was boldly visible in dark-brown script trimmed with gold.

"I couldn't make out the name from the shore," confessed Angie.

"It had only two words," said Jess, frowning.

"The second word was *Sea*."

While Angie stood puzzling, Jess strode down the planked walkway alongside *The Blowing Clear* and hopped aboard. He reached over the fish well and ran his hand along the dark letters, probing with his fingers.

"Hello," he said, and tugged at something. He held up a scrap no bigger than a postage stamp.

"Tape," he said. He turned thoughtfully toward the bow. "I wonder. . . ."

Without another word, he went forward and felt along the registration numbers on the bow. When he straightened, he held another scrap of tape pinched between thumb and forefinger.

The two pieces of tape, left sticking carelessly, told a fascinating story. When *The Blowing Clear* has passed Seaward Island, another name and another set of registration numbers had covered the real ones.

Angie joined Jess on board. Together they looked for what they hoped they would not find — bloodstains.

The deck was spotless.

"They've had time to wash everything down," commented Jess.

Angie pictured the shooting. After the gunshot, one of the men had clutched his chest with both hands, staggered, and grabbed at the ladder to the flybridge.

She examined the ladder. It shone with the lus-

66

ter of a fresh polishing. Reaching behind the rails, where a cleaning rag might miss, she rubbed upward, and felt a wet spot.

Her hand recoiled. A smear of reddish fluid lay on her forefinger.

"B-blood would have dried by now, wouldn't it?" she stammered, holding out her hand.

Jess touched the reddish fluid and sniffed. "Transmission oil," he announced. He shook his head long and slowly. "It had me fooled. It sure looked like blood through the binoculars."

"It was meant to," said Angie. "Why?"

"We wasted half a day solving a murder in which no one was killed," Jess said half to himself. "But I guess it'll be good news to the Coast Guard."

"Why should they go to such trouble to fake a shooting?" Angie pondered.

"I'd say they didn't catch any fish and were bored," replied Jess. "So they dreamed up the stunt to amuse themselves."

"Talk about a twisted sense of humor," Angie said.

"That sums it up nicely," Jess said. "No crime has been committed except by us. We came aboard without permission."

He climbed onto the walkway. Then, needing to release his disgust, he flung a loud "Phooey!" at the boat.

As they headed out the gate, Angie felt that fate was treating her attempt to be a detective like a straw in the wind. After nearly four weeks, her efforts had come to nothing. Instead of finding the Wolfpack, she had stumbled on a pen thief and escaped the frightening pursuit of a mystery man. Now she had uncovered a prank that made no sense.

She was brooding on these misadventures when a gleaming black car pulled up scarcely six feet away. Two men jumped out. The movements were all so swift and startling that nothing else registered on Angie: neither the faces of the men nor the fact that one wore a red shirt and the other a sleeveless undershirt.

The men got behind her and Jess. An instant later Angie lifted onto her toes in pain and terror. A strong hand had clasped the back of her neck.

"Get into the car, kids," the man behind her ordered. He squeezed her neck once, hard.

The other man had Jess by the arm. "Nobody'll get hurt."

Before she could think, Angie found herself packed into the seat next to Jess. The men sat flanking them.

The driver, alone in the front seat, started the engine. He wore a blue shirt, and Angie guessed he had been the man on the flybridge of *The Blowing Clear*. The other two had been with him.

*They're carrying a prank too far*, she thought, with more resentment than fear.

Then the driver turned around, and Angie

stared at him wildly. It was he . . . the man who had worn the tan suit . . . the mystery man!

From a yard away, he looked younger than she remembered him. His face was handsome and rough-hewn, with a square jaw above an athlete's neck. But his eyes were wrong—wrong for any face. They were pale blue and queerly without depth, like shutters, not windows, to the mind.

"You," he grunted at Angie. "What's your name?"

"Gladys," Angie answered. "Gladys Fransworth."

"Where do you live, Gladys Fransworth?"

"Palm View Towers," Angie replied without hesitation. Palm View Towers was a swank new complex in Miami. It crawled with the emblems of luxury—private guards and enough walls, locks, and alarms to stymie snoopers till November.

"And you, tubby?"

Jess said, "Jerry Fransworth. I'm her twin brother."

"They could be lying," groused the man by Jess.

"We'll find out," the mystery man said ominously. "In the meantime, we'll have to stash them."

The blindfold went on, smelling of marine oil. Angie crinkled the corners of her eyes to make the flesh puff. Before the darkness, she caught a fleeting glimpse of Jess, bulging a little in his striped shirt. He sat calmly, his arms folded across his chest with determined self-possession.

*He doesn't know who's driving*, Angie thought, even as she drew a measure of strength from his composure. *And I'm not going to worry him.*

A gag was stuffed into her mouth and pulled tightly behind her head below the blindfold. She choked for several seconds before she could breathe again.

"Ready?" said the mystery man.

"Another second," said the man by Jess.

Angie held herself very carefully. She remembered movies in which the hero was kidnapped and blindfolded. Yet he outwitted his captors by employing his other senses to the utmost. Later, he was able to retrace the route to the villains' hideout and bag the whole lot of them.

In the movies it was easy. There were always special sounds that earmarked the line of travel: the wheezing clangor of a train, the shrill whistle of a ferry, the chimes of churchbells — plus smells, changes of temperature, and the passage of time.

Angie cleared her mind for the demanding task ahead. The car moved forward and picked up speed.

She began to count: "One thousand and one, one thousand and two . . ." When they reached their destination, she would know the number of seconds the trip had taken.

The stops and turns, now. She kept track of

them while counting the seconds. For a long time, she distinguished between the right turns and the left turns, between the long stops (traffic lights) and the short (stop signs).

She juggled the individual counts till the car swerved to the right and then straightened unexpectedly. She had to erase a right turn, and the correction threw her off. The partitions of her mind quivered and collapsed. All the numbers — of seconds, turns, stops — flooded together meaninglessly.

To start over was pointless. *Listen*, she scolded herself. *Listen*.

The only sounds blared from the car radio. With the windows up and the air-conditioner and radio on, an ambulance with a siren wailing might have driven over her feet before she heard it. *Movie heroes are never kidnapped in hot weather*, she concluded.

The car slowed, made a right turn, and stopped smoothly.

"Out," the man next to her said.

She groped from the car. A hand fell on her shoulder and guided her.

It was now or never.

She sneezed. It hurt with the gag in her mouth, but she sneezed twice more and yanked out her handkerchief. The pennies clinked musically on the paved ground.

*That ought to fake them out for a minute*, she thought.

Blanketing her face with the handkerchief, she sneezed again for good measure. As she did, she poked one finger under the handkerchief and pushed up. The blindfold moved a slit. Enough.

She was standing in the yard of an auto body shop. Two vans were parked in the open stalls immediately in front of her. One was white with the rear doors, bumper, and taillights missing. The other was shiny maroon. Above the stalls was painted the name V.J. Donovan and Sons, Inc.

"Lock them in the storeroom," a man's voice commanded.

# Chapter
# 8

A door scraped on squeaky hinges. The hand on Angie's shoulder thrust her forward.

Jess banged blindly into her back, and they went down in a leg-weaving heap. The door slammed. A key echoed in the lock.

"Stay put and be quiet," a man said from the other side of the door.

Angie and Jess untangled themselves and tore off the blindfolds and gags.

"Are you hurt?" Jess asked.

"A few bruises is all," replied Angie. "How about you?"

"Knocked my elbow," Jess said. "My funny bone feels like a laughing hyena sank his teeth into it."

"It's lucky we didn't crack our skulls," Angie said, looking around.

The room that held them prisoner was small and as tidy as a baby junkyard. Rusting auto parts lay piled against the walls. A sprinkling of empty paint cans added forlorn touches of color to the aging jumble.

"A natural beauty spot," Jess commented. "A holiday place complete with souvenirs."

"It looks like my room on Sunday night," Angie said.

The window offered no escape. It was criss-crossed with bars. The view was of dirty, one-story warehouses.

"I think we're somewhere in Miami," Angie declared. "Where are the binoculars?"

"Ask Mr. Red Shirt," Jess said. "He stole them first thing."

"Never mind. We won't need them," Angie said.

A young man lugging a steel storm shutter appeared outside the window. "Watch yourself, kid," he declared.

He hoisted the shutter and fastened it with a great amount of heaving, pounding, and cursing. The room was steeped in dungeonlike darkness.

"All that's missing is a moat and drawbridge," Jess quipped, groping for the light.

"They shouldn't treat important prisoners like this," said Angie, doing her best to match Jess's humor.

"The room service may be better," Jess countered.

"Bread and water is bread and water," Angie managed.

Jess found the light switch and flicked it on. He tested the door, jiggling the knob and pushing. No soap. He examined the lock with his face screwed up.

"Mmmm . . ." he said. "I might be able to open it."

"Now isn't the time," Angie cautioned. "We'd just walk straight into their arms."

She wished she had kept silent. A flutter in her voice had betrayed her. She forced herself to speak in a calm, formal tone. Without fright. "How long do you think they will keep us here?"

"If I knew *why* they kidnapped us, I might be able to guess the answer," Jess replied.

Angie said, "They didn't lock us up for boarding *The Blowing Clear*. It has to be something else...."

"Relax," Jess said. "They have no reason to hurt us."

He fell to throwing aside rusty auto parts — gears, shafts, manifolds — and soon had cleared a respectable place against one wall. Using a blindfold, he wiped the floor for them to sit down.

"We might as well make ourselves comfortable," he said.

Angie sat beside him. Their shoulders touched, and Jess took her hand and gave it a quick squeeze. Angie squeezed back, telling him she was all right.

"Gladys Fransworth," Jess mused. "Where'd you get that name?"

"From a book," Angie answered. "She was the heroine and neat and tidy as a pin. Her room always looked like a furniture-store window, night and day. She didn't have an enemy in the world. Everyone loved her."

"Except you."

"She deserved to be kidnapped," Angie said.

The rough voices of the men outside reached them in fits and snatches. The talk was of bumpers and fenders, motor sizes and prices. By piecing together bits of conversation, Angie came to understand the manner of place in which they were being held. "This is a chop shop," she said.

"What's that?"

"An auto body shop that specializes in stolen cars," Angie explained. "Kit told me about them. They strip cars and sell the parts."

"Chop shop...." Jess rolled the name on his tongue as if readying a quip. He said nothing but merely stared at his hands.

For a long time they sat in total silence. The power to toss off the wisecracks that had supported them was spent. Silently they battled to hold up against what was happening, against the hideous metal graveyard of a room that made it all so immediate and terrifyingly real.

Angie shut her eyes and clung fast to thoughts of Aunt Velma and Kit. By now Aunt Velma would be growing anxious about her. Angie pictured Aunt Velma in the living room, glancing at the clock and rubbing her fingers along the arms of her chair.

And Kit . . . Kit to the rescue? That was asking the impossible. Kit could handle almost any situation — sudden ones like speeding violations, dangerous ones like holdups. And she could work steadily and patiently, as in tracking down the ring of counterfeiters. But the kidnapping defied patience and courage and ability. There was nothing to go on.

Fear pounded at Angie's mind and focused it on her shortcomings. "If I ever get out of this, I'll pick up everything," she vowed. "No more mess."

"You say something?"

"Huh?"

"You were mumbling," Jess asserted. "Want to play twenty questions?"

They played twenty questions. They played every word game they could think of, plus a few rounds of two-headed duck-duck-goose. By eight o'clock, when the room had got hot enough to please a moth and Angie had lost count of the games they had played, the door opened. Red Shirt tossed a brown paper bag at Jess.

"Your dinner," he said. "We're closing. Charlie will be here all night. So stay put. See you in the morning."

In the bag were two hamburgers and two chocolate milkshakes.

"Hungry?" Jess inquired.

"No," Angie said. The fuzzy-dry taste of the gag had stuck on her tongue.

Outside the men were bidding one another good night. Their voices gradually trailed off. A car started up, followed by several others. The motors blended into a harsh melody of pistons and exhausts. Tires squealed. Then a deep quiet settled over everything.

"What do you think is going to happen?" Angie asked.

"Strike me if I know," returned Jess. "Obviously, Charlie is supposed to keep us here all night."

"We've got to break out before morning," Angie said. "Before they figure out what to do with us."

Jess was absorbed in digging among the heaps of useless old auto parts. He chose a connecting rod and swung it like a hatchet.

"Angie," he said slowly, "shout for Charlie. When he pokes his head in, I'll bop him a good one."

"For heaven's sake, no!" Angie cried. "You might kill him!"

"Then I'll bop him a good one on the shin. While he's hopping around and hollering, we can run for it."

Angie stood up nervously. She felt the outline of her spine sharply against the skin of her back. "Okay . . ." She licked her lips and filled her lungs.

"Charlee!" she shouted. "Charleee!"

No answer.

"Charlie...! Charlie!" she shouted, till her throat hurt.

"Don't stop," Jess begged.

"I — I have to," Angie said weakly. "I can't shout 'Charlie' one more time. My voice is giving out."

"Try hollering 'Chuck,' " Jess suggested. "It's only one syllable."

"Chuck!" Angie squeaked once.

Jess was on one knee with his ear to the keyhole. He looked puzzled. "There's no one walking around outside."

He proceeded to search the room. He found what he wanted hanging from a nail, a dipstick. "That old lock belongs on a closet," he said. "Easy pickings."

In a matter of seconds, Angie heard the key fall on the other side. Then Jess uttered an exclamation of glee as the lock tumbled. He inched the door open. Angie came up and looked with him through the widening crack.

The security lights were on. They could see that a six-foot concrete wall enclosed the yard. To the left were the open stalls that Angie had seen on the way in. The two vans, the white and the maroon, were still parked there.

Jess picked up a camshaft and gave it to Angie.

"Just in case," he said. "The gate will be chained. We'll have to scale the wall. Think you can?"

Angie managed a yes.

"Scared?"

"And how," she whispered. Fear and excitement heated her face like flames.

"Me, too," confessed Jess. "Here we go."

He pushed the door open and took two steps shortened by caution. Right behind him, Angie had taken a step and was shifting her weight for another, when a shadow moved.

Only a sixth sense stayed Jess from walking out beyond the point of no retreat. For at first the movement was merely an innocent-looking ripple in a pool of shadows, a slight stirring glimpsed uncertainly.

But it grew with miraculous speed, detaching itself from the mother shadow cast by a wrecked delivery truck. Racing across the asphalt of the courtyard, it assumed the solid shape of a Doberman pinscher.

The lights caught the patches of tan in the sleek black hide, the gleam of savage eyes, and in front of the eyes a terrible pink wetness of jaws and the glint of fangs. Straight for Angie and Jess the black dog raced, its crazed barking a tumult in the night air.

Angie was bowled over as Jess flung her back into the room and slammed the door.

"Charlie!" he gasped through whitened lips.

Angie lay where she had fallen. She trembled in every muscle.

The door suddenly seemed too old and rickety to withstand the Doberman. In the frenzy to get at them, he had stood up on his hind legs. Angie heard his claws scratching high up on the wood.

The assault did not last long. Foiled, Charlie soon stopped his fierce clawing. The wildly furious barks turned into resentful growls and high, nervous whines of canine frustration.

Jess put his eye to the keyhole. "He's sitting down...about ten feet away. He's watching the door like a cobra."

"We can't stay here," Angie said. "Those men won't keep us locked up the rest of our lives. Tomorrow they'll have to do something. We've got to get away tonight."

"I've been thinking along those very lines," said Jess unhappily. "But Charlie is chomping at my concentration."

Angie reached into the paper dinner bag. She lifted out a milkshake and removed the top of the container.

"Now what?" Jess said.

"I'm going to bribe him," she replied. "Charlie must be awfuly thirsty after all that yapping."

"He doesn't strike me as the ice-cream-parlor type," Jess said.

Angie peeked through the keyhole. The Doberman was lying on his belly. His proud, lean head was raised alertly to the door.

Angie pressed the door open just far enough to set down the milkshake. She spilled some in her haste to pull back her arm.

Immediately the din of barking resumed, but it

was short-lived. Angie heard slurping, and then the hollow-pitched tones of the empty container overturning and rolling.

"He drank it!" she yelped with glee.

"I had him wrong," Jess said. "He's really a fun fellow. Another drink and we'll sing *Havenue Sholemaleichem* together." He put out the other milkshake.

Charlie was no longer thirsty. Or he remembered his duty. Whichever, he ignored the milkshake and did his best to snap off Jess's hand.

"That's one mean mutt," Jess observed.

"He's hungry now," Angie corrected.

"Let him nibble on someone else's hand," Jess said. "I've only got two."

"We can use a hungry Charlie," Angie said.

Jess didn't understand. "Your imagination is showing again," he said.

"You should be glad of it," Angie retorted.

It was impossible to slip past Charlie and climb the wall. But it might be possible to get out of the little room and hide somewhere else.

She said, "If the men don't find us in here tomorrow morning, they'll think we escaped."

"Or Charlie ate us."

"There are two vans outside," Angie went on. "A white van with the back doors missing, and a maroon van. The maroon van isn't fifteen feet away. We can hide in it."

"Charlie won't cooperate," objected Jess.

"We have hamburgers," Angie said. "If we can lure him far enough away from the door, we can make a dash for the maroon van."

"You must be rubbing off on me. I'm beginning to follow you," Jess said. "There's a chance the van will be driven off tomorrow with us hiding in the back. Is that the scheme?"

"It's our *only* chance."

Jess stared at the brown paper bag. "May Charlie boy like hamburgers better than kids," he said prayerfully.

# Chapter
# 9

They didn't argue about who would attempt to lead Charlie away — away from the door and away from the maroon van. The job indisputably fell to Jess. He was better at throwing, and a good arm was what counted now.

Angie took a hamburger from the brown bag and broke off a piece. Jess received it gravely. He listened, bending his head to the door, and then opened it a slit. With a baseball catcher's quick release, he flipped the meat about six feet.

Charlie sprang the instant the door moved. Only Jess's quickness enabled him to avoid the strong white teeth. Angie flinched, for the dog's presence ripped through the flimsy old door in savage sounds and seething energy.

Eventually the crash of barking died down. Jess, at the keyhole, reported: "He's turning away. . . . He's eating the meat!"

Angie breathed with relief. The first vital step had succeeded. The war between cunning and savagery was on.

Each time Jess threw out a piece of hamburger, he slammed the door as loudly as he could. Charlie, after the door had slammed, trotted to where the meat had fallen.

Charlie had to learn the point of it all: The rules did not change. The door would open, the meat would fly out, and the door would slam shut. Simple. There was nothing else. Through repetition, the dog had to be convinced that his prisoners would stay where they were after the meat was thrown and the door shut.

Gradually Jess worked the Doberman farther and farther from the door and the van. After the sixth throw, he had good news. Charlie had chased the meat halfway to the wall.

"Break the other hamburger in two," he said. "We can't drag this out. Charlie may lose interest."

Angie's throat had begun to choke up, but she did as Jess instructed. They were getting near it.

The deadly game seemed to be progressing perfectly, when it brushed disaster. As Jess threw, his hand on the doorknob slipped. In that fraction of a delay, Charlie wedged his snout into the opening. The unmuffled barks crashed terrifyingly into the small room. Before Jess could fight the door closed, Angie felt the raw, powerful force that was the dog's will to seize and destroy.

Jess slumped with his back against the door, his face pale. Angie waited until he motioned before handing him the last piece of hamburger. She clutched her weapon, the camshaft, with both hands. Awkward and heavy, it would be difficult to swing accurately.

Jess wadded the meat into a ball and leaned his connecting rod against the door frame.

"Ready?" he whispered.

"Ready."

The thought crossed Angie's mind that the throw had to be perfect. If it was, they had a chance; Charlie would have to streak one hundred and fifty feet to the maroon van while they covered fifteen. If the meat fell short of the wall. . . .

Jess said, "When the meat strikes the ground, it will break up. Charlie will sniff out the pieces, and that should give us an extra second or two."

He stood up, one hand on the doorknob and the other clutching the meat. "Here goes."

His body arched as the door opened. His arm whipped forward.

The door slammed before Charlie could get at them. He raged for a minute, then quieted. He had turned his attention once more to the meat.

Jess withdrew from the keyhole and uttered a single word: "*Now!*"

It was too late to worry about the tattling squeak of the hinges. Jess was out of the room and sprinting. He lunged at the driver's door of the maroon van and yanked it wide.

"Jump in!" he urged frantically.

Angie dropped the camshaft even as the first low grumble rose from the shadows by the wall. Charlie had seen them, and Charlie was coming.

Angie dived past the steering wheel and squirmed onto the passenger seat beyond. She tucked her legs up tight to give Jess every spare inch.

"Jess!"

The torrent of barks drowned out her voice and engulfed the van. She saw the sinewy black form leap a barrier of three tires and suddenly vanish.

"Jess, hurry!"

Something struck her foot, and she shrieked in terror. It was Jess's shoulder. He had bellied onto the driver's seat. He lay with his head touching the floor and his feet scuffing the headliner.

Charlie loomed up, jaws snapping viciously. The eyes, of darkest brown, glowed fiendishly in the black head. But he came no nearer. The thin pane of window glass thwarted him. Somehow, Jess had managed to bang the door in his face.

"That," gasped Jess, "is no Sugar Plum Fairy."

The Doberman disappeared from Jess's window only to rear up with unreduced fury at Angie's. Unable to force an entry, he dropped to all fours. He prowled about the van, twice circling it as he hunted a way in.

Angie and Jess shifted up to a sitting position and sat without speaking. They allowed themselves a spell of gratitude for being safe and whole and alive.

Jess spoke first. "We'll have to spend the night like this. There's nothing back there but hard floor."

Angie twisted around. The van was built for deliveries. It had no rear seats or carpeting. The sides and floor were bare metal, painted yellow.

*There's no place to hide*, she thought.

"Charlie's given up," Jess said. "Get some sleep."

Angie closed her eyes. But in her mind she kept seeing Charlie's jaws and the empty rear of the van.

"Jess, something's wrong."

He chuckled. "You noticed?"

"I mean, do you smell fresh paint?"

"And how. We're in a paint and body shop."

Angie carefully lowered her window a couple of inches. She sniffed.

"The maroon paint," she said. "It's new. It still smells."

"So the owner had the van painted," Jess said. "That's a crime only if you don't like maroon."

Angie held her tongue. She leaned back in the bucket seat and closed her eyes again. She wanted to tell Jess what she was thinking. There was no need, however, to add to his worries. Even if she was right, there was nothing he could do about it now.

Throughout the long, hot, wearying night she glanced at him frequently. He sat motionless, eyes closed. For her benefit he was faking sleep; he was pretending the danger was too small to spoil his rest.

At dawn she jabbed his ribs and pointed. Charlie had awakened.

The black dog rose, pulling backward drowsily from outstretched legs. Ignoring the van, he padded elegantly to a bowl of water. After lapping his fill, he returned to his place and settled down with head snugly between forepaws.

At seven o'clock a truck braked outside the gate. Angie and Jess scrambled into the rear of the van and curled up on the hard floor, behind the seats. The gate ground open. The truck drove in.

Other vehicles arrived. The auto body shop came alive with the ring of voices, machines, and tools. The talk was mainly about the cars to be worked on and girlfriends.

At seven-twenty, the escape was discovered. The voices swelled in alarm. The men were angry, and their anger was directed at someone named Jeeter.

Jeeter, Angie gathered, was not employed at the shop. Apparently he was one of the three men who had kidnapped her and Jess.

A deep bass voice began spraying orders. Jeeter

had to be informed. The hot cars had to be moved. The place had to be shaped up. "Them kids will have the cops busting in here any second."

A blond man got behind the wheel of the maroon van and started the engine.

"Hold it, Ed," the deep voice shouted. "Here comes Warren."

As Ed slid from the van, a new and youthful voice called: "What's going on?"

"Never mind. Just get in and go," the deep voice ordered.

"Is she finished?"

"Finished enough. Get 'er outa here!"

"Lemme have the bill, and I'll — "

"Pay me come Christmas. We've got trouble. Move her!"

Warren plunked himself behind the steering wheel. "Ciao, you all," he sang cockily.

He drove smoothly and expertly. Angie scarcely was aware of the stops and turns. After several minutes she felt the van slow. The passenger door opened before the wheels had fully stopped.

"Going my way, Kurt, old buddy?" Warren said, a grin in his tone.

"You're off schedule — twelve seconds early," Kurt proclaimed, taking his seat. "That's not like you."

"Old man Donovan didn't charge for the paint job," Warren said. "He threw my timing off."

"The maroon is free?"

"Why not? Donovan loves us, buddy. Didn't you know?" Warren laughed. "Naw, he was acting like he had a boil on his head."

"Trouble?"

"Yeah — his, not ours. I didn't hang around to find out his problem and hold his hand."

"What about Sonny?"

"Scratch him. His ankle is still puffed up like a grapefruit. He can't walk, let alone drive."

"I don't like it," Kurt said. "Only the two of us."

"Two is enough. Just the coin collection today. Nothing heavy. Heather has it all laid out."

"Heather better be sure of this one," Kurt remarked.

"Take it easy," Warren said. He braked for a traffic light. "Heather is a regular little army scout in maid's clothing."

"And the Bronsons' maid?"

"A skinny old broad named Zelda. Heather's drunk enough coffee with her this week to float a stone battleship. Zelda's daughter is being married this afternoon. Proud Mamma will be gone all day. The house is empty."

"Suppose her people come home?"

"No way. They'll be in Maine the rest of the month. I trailed them to the airport myself and watched them board the plane for Lewiston."

"I don't like going out this early," Kurt said. "We never did it before."

"First time for everything," Warren replied.

"Besides, Heather knows what she's doing."

"I got this feeling," Kurt said uncomfortably.

"Hang loose, buddy," Warren encouraged. "After this morning, every day will be like New Year's Eve. Heather and I might scoot off to Colorado."

"Pulling two jobs on Seaward Island in a week has me jumpy," Kurt confessed. "I'm glad this is the last."

"Amen to that," Warren breathed. "From tomorrow on, it's good-bye to grease guns and 'Have a nice day, sir.' You're going to see the real me."

"So long to army and navy stores forever," said Kurt.

The pair chortled, and their conversation veered to the heady pleasures of sudden wealth.

Angie ceased to listen. Jess was staring at her. Silently his lips formed the word: "Wolfpack." Angie nodded knowingly.

From the moment she had spied the yellow inside walls and floor of the van, she had suspected it. This was the yellow van that had been seen in front of the Weygand house the morning of the robbery.

Angie's heart sank. After nearly a month of hunting the gang of teenagers, she had found them. And she was in no position to do anything about it.

# Chapter
# 10

Looking up from the floor of the van, Angie saw the outside world through the windows in the rear doors. Mostly she saw chunks of sky, though now and then a building higher than one story streaked by.

She could not get her bearings till Warren drove past the tower of the Federal Loan Association office. She recognized it by the electric weather and time sign near the top. So . . . the van was moving along Tropical Avenue.

By means of hand language, she and Jess settled on a course of action. When the van stopped at the next traffic light, they would bolt for the rear doors.

The van did not stop, however. The traffic lights on Tropical Avenue lit in sequence, and Warren maintained the speed necessary to stay apace of the greens. The last hope was the traffic light at the Whitehorse Bridge; it operated independently of the others. But Warren made that one, too. He turned left, and Angie knew they were crossing the bridge.

Seaward Island had no traffic lights, only stop signs and yield signs. She and Jess would have to keep down until Warren parked in front of the home that had been targeted for robbery.

"How much farther?" Kurt asked.

"It's that wood colonial," Warren answered.

The van slowed and swung off the road. Angie felt the slight jar as it dipped onto the driveway and then stopped.

"The coin collection is in the study," Warren said. "You might as well check the vanity in the master bedroom. Who the — "

Both youths made gurgling noises of disbelief. Angie and Jess were at the rear doors struggling with the handles.

Warren jumped from the van. When Angie finally pushed her door open, he was barring the way. "Who the devil are you?" he said, dumbfounded.

Angie and Jess sat down in defeat. Angie rubbed her head where she had bumped it against the low ceiling.

"C'mon, give," demanded Kurt, who was stooping between the front seats. He had a narrow, nervous face, as if he'd spent his life peeping into other people's mail. "Who are you?"

Neither Angie nor Jess replied. They huddled together on the floor of the van, trapped between two members of the Wolfpack.

"Let's hear it," said Warren grimly. He looked like an ex-high-school football star who had run out of seasons.

"We've taken a vow of silence," Jess croaked.

"You bucking for a humor award?" Kurt said. He reached over the seat to yank Jess's hair but came up short.

"All right," Angie said. "We're runaways. We're going to California."

"We needed a place for the night," Jess added. "It looked like rain."

"Peddle that someplace else," Kurt said menacingly. "Nobody sneaks past the attack dog at Donovan's."

"Well, we did," Angie retorted. "See for yourself."

The two youths stared at the stowaways in rage and dismay. Kurt seemed on the verge of flinging himself on them.

Warren said, "I want some answers. I don't have all day."

"We're secret agents working on an important case," Angie confessed.

"We're with the juvenile division of the FBI," Jess said. "Our mission is classified. You can torture us and we won't spill a word."

"They're crazy, whacko!" blurted Kurt, who seemed about to come undone. He looked wildly at Warren. "What a lousy break! What'll we do?"

"Keep your head," Warren rebuked him. He glanced anxiously about. Every minute of delay increased the danger of discovery.

"We can't stay out here," Kurt said frantically.

"I'm not about to call this off," Warren said. "We'll take them inside." He seized Angie. "One noise out of either of you and you'll wish you'd been born an oyster in Japan."

He twisted Angie's arm behind her back. Swiftly he marched her around the house to the rear door. Kurt, who had Jess wincing in a similar grip, seemed to enjoy applying pressure.

"Let's have no hard feelings, eh, fellows?" Jess gasped.

Warren drew out a case of lock picks from his hip pocket. He gave Angie to Kurt and went to work on the door with professional skill. The lock yielded to the second pick.

"Inside," he ordered.

Angie heard voices. Her hopes fluttered briefly, then died. The voices were part of a beer commercial. The television had been left on in the empty house to scare off burglars.

Warren shepherded Angie and Jess into the living room. "Watch them, not the television," he told Kurt, and went in search of the study and the coin collection.

The living room was divided into two seating areas. One area consisted of two easy chairs grouped in front of the television set near the entrance. The other, at the far end of the large room, had two white love seats facing each other at right angles to a fireplace. Between the love seats stood a glass-topped coffee table.

"You two kids kneel on that one," Kurt directed.

As she walked to the love seat to which Kurt pointed, Angie took in the room. Kurt seated himself in a leather armchair against the wall, abreast of the love seats. Above his head was a cuckoo clock. The hands pointed to seven minutes before eight.

Angie arranged the future in her imagination. In seven minutes the mechanical cuckoo would pop out and cry the hour in a piping, woodwind voice. For a second or two, Kurt's attention would be drawn to it. For a second or two, he would look away. . . . Seven minutes.

Angie and Jess knelt obediently on the love seat, their backs to Kurt. With the television going, it was possible for them to whisper without being overheard.

They used up three minutes debating their move. Jess didn't like Angie's role and wanted to swap. Angie insisted on having her way. Kurt and Warren, she maintained, would more readily believe that a boy had escaped than a girl. She would be the decoy.

They waited, eyes on their wristwatches. At four minutes before the hour, Warren returned, carrying a leatherbound coin case. He was beside himself.

"Look," he bubbled. "The old boy kept *this* in a crackerbox home safe!"

"Heather was right?" Kurt asked eagerly.

"She wasn't right enough," Warren replied. "There are three two-cent pieces dated 1864 and a three-cent Liberty Head. And that's only the cheap stuff."

"What do you think it's worth?"

"Enough to rebuild New York City," Warren replied. "These two been behaving themselves?"

"Quiet as mice," Kurt answered.

"Keep your eyes on them," Warren said. "I'm going to look upstairs. If the old boy can play with coins like these, his old lady ought to have more gold trinkets than King Tut."

"We got what we came for," Kurt said. "Let's get out of here."

"Don't go antsy on me now," Warren said. "You just watch Hansel and Gretel, and I'll buy you a gingerbread house the size of the Lincoln Memorial."

Kurt sat down resignedly under the cuckoo clock. Angie heard Warren's footsteps mounting the stairs. It was one minute before eight.

The minute passed like ten. Angie watched the second hand sweep around the face of her wristwatch. At eight o'clock it passed the twelve and descended toward the six.

"The cuckoo isn't working," she thought in despair.

Then suddenly it came, first a *whisssh-clunk* of the tiny wood plank falling into place, and then a trumpeting *cuckoo!*

Before the first cuckoo had faded, Jess was diving over the back of the love seat. Angie spun off the cushions and darted for the living room entrance. Kurt shouted and caught her in the foyer.

"Run, Jess!" she cried, in the general direction of the back door.

Kurt slapped a hand over her mouth and wrestled her motionless.

Warren appeared at the top of the staircase. "Where's the butterball?"

"I think he got away," Kurt replied, abashed.

Warren hastened down the stairs. "Maybe he's hiding."

"He got away," Kurt repeated, but he did not admit he had watched the two prisoners every second.

Warren cursed. "It's time to call it quits."

"What about her?"

"Leave her here. She can't do any harm."

"That butterball," Kurt said. "He'll be at a telephone any second. It'll take us three or four minutes to reach the bridge. The cops will be waiting for us."

"We'll pick up Heather on the way and use her car," Warren said. He hurried into the kitchen.

Kurt bent Angie's arm behind her back with enthusiasm. "One scream and I'll break it off," he warned, pushing her into the kitchen.

Warren was at the telephone. He spoke tersely. "We're done, honey. Wait for us in your car, and have the motor running. Yes, fine. . . . No . . . No. We'll be there in two, three minutes."

Instead of hanging up, he wrenched the phone from the wall. He tied Angie's hands and feet with dish towels. Kurt gagged her.

"She'll keep for ten minutes," Warren said. "Then it won't matter. By the time the cops stop looking for a maroon van, we'll be halfway to Georgia." He snatched up the coin collection and the pair ran out.

Jess came in from the living room where he'd been hiding behind the love seat. "Call the police!" Angie bawled as soon he had removed her gag. "You can free me later." She rattled off the number, and Jess went in search of a working telephone.

She had squirmed off the floor and was sitting on a chair when he returned.

"The desk officer knew all about you," he said, marveling. "Your sister has the whole force on the alert."

"Is Kit coming?"

"The officer didn't say. But he knew the call

wasn't a prank. Kit put your name on the missing persons' list."

"If Kit is assigned the case, she'll stomp on the Wolfpack but good," Angie said.

She envisioned the capture: Kit advancing on the getaway car; Kit scooping Heather from behind the wheel; Kit twirling Warren and Kurt into a deep swoon; Kit slapping handcuffs on all three.

"If Kit's sent on the case, I hope she has some backup," Jess said, untying Angie's feet.

"Kit can handle three teenagers," Angie assured him.

Jess smiled. "If Kit's muscles are as powerful as your imagination, I don't envy Warren and Kurt."

He opened the refrigerator and examined the contents for nibbles. "Hungry?" he inquired. "We've done these folks a good turn, and one good turn deserves another, I say."

Angie remembered that her last meal had been breakfast, twenty-four hours ago. "I'm starved," she said. "Would you mind untying my hands?"

# Chapter
# 11

Aunt Velma wanted to meet Jess. "You should invite him over for dinner," she said, laying the casserole of jambalaya, Angie's favorite dish, on the table.

They were eating in the dining room instead of the kitchen. For the occasion, the table was laid with the good silverware and china. A majestic celebration cake rested like a crown on the buffet.

"Jess is a brave boy," Aunt Velma said.

"Angie didn't do so badly," Kit commented.

"What more can I say about Angie?" Aunt Velma replied. "The only reason I stopped kissing her was to prepare dinner."

"She never gave up," Kit remarked. "She jogged the streets of Dadesville for nearly a month."

"And ended up a prisoner of the Wolfpack," Angie said, forcing a grin.

Despite Aunt Velma and Kit's festive humor, Angie's mood was strained. Oh, yes, the Wolfpack had been caught. The police stopped the gang at the Whitehorse Bridge. Heather, still in her maid's uniform, was driving her own car. Warren was with her, and Kurt was hiding in the trunk compartment. Sonny, the fourth and absent member of the gang, was taken at his home a few hours later. And the men at the auto body shop were booked for dealing in stolen autos. But Kit hadn't been among the arresting officers.

"Nobody at the station figured on Heather," Kit said. "We didn't get any reports of a girl running with the Wolfpack."

"She didn't run with them—she *ran* them," said Angie, quoting a remark she had overheard at the station. "When I went to identify Warren and Kurt, she acted real tough. She tried to spit on me."

Kit looked questioningly at Angie. "You don't seem to be enjoying your hour of triumph."

"I'm enjoying it," Angie said. And to some extent she was. The case had been wrapped up. At least the case of the Wolfpack had been. The three men who had stolen the sport fisherman were still at large. The station captain had wired their descriptions to the police of surrounding communities.

Angie and Jess were heroes. The officers had doted on them. Newspaper reporters had cor-

nered them for half an hour, and then a man
from a mobile TV unit had taped an interview
for the eleven o'clock news. But Kit had been left
out of it, and so the taste of victory had a bitter
tinge.

When Jess's telephone call came into the station,
Kit was in area two, three miles from Seaward
Island, writing out a traffic ticket. She missed
the capture of the Wolfpack completely. Not a
jot of credit went on her service record, for all of
Angie's derring-do.

Angie tried to put on a bright face, but she could
not mask her feelings. Not from Kit.

"Be proud of what you did—for your own sake,"
Kit said.

"It didn't turn out the way I'd hoped," Angie
replied. "You know that."

"I know," Kit said with a tender smile.

Aunt Velma finished serving the jambalaya. She
chattered gaily about the number of people she had
told to watch the eleven o'clock news.

Listening to Aunt Velma's happy voice, and being surrounded by love and approval, Angie began
to relax for the first time in hours. The disappointment about Kit's role notwithstanding, her
thoughts drifted pleasantly and aimlessly.

The wild and scary events of the past few days
paled and merged and sank below her conscious
thoughts. She let her mind go blank, and blankly it
waited, ripe for fresh impressions.

It was precisely then that Aunt Velma said something. A spot deep within Angie's brain twitched, as if it had been sharply pricked. She stammered, "S-say that again."

"Say what again?" Aunt Velma inquired.

"You said something just now. Say it again."

Aunt Velma knitted her brow. "Well . . . I think I said half of Dadesville will be glued to channel three tonight."

"Three!" Angie heard herself cry out.

The number bounded back and forth in her head. Pictures and thoughts rose and swirled crazily. A few, which had formerly been unconnected, began to attract one another and fit together.

"Kit, the counterfeiters! We can capture them!" Angie cried excitedly.

Kit and Aunt Velma sat very still, as they always did when Angie's imagination broke loose.

"Don't stare at me like that," Angie protested. "I tell you I know—almost." She looked earnestly at Kit. "You've been hunting the counterfeiters, haven't you? You told me so!"

Kit nodded. "Another phony twenty showed up in Dadesville yesterday. The bills are being passed in a trickle, four or five a week. That makes tracking them down extremely difficult."

"I can find the place where the printing plates are kept," Angie said.

Kit looked up from her food. Her attitude hovered between curiosity and disbelief. "You're sure?"

"Almost."

"Almost?" Kit said.

Aunt Velma interceded. "Angie helped capture the Wolfpack, Kit. Why not trust her?"

"Because she's guessing," Kit anwered predictably.

Angie dropped her head lower and lower, not knowing how to counter what was coming. She was inches from putting everything together, but without Kit's help she might never succeed.

"I'm almost sure, and that's sure enough," Angie said doggedly. "I can't explain until I have the printing plates."

"Honestly, Angie," Kit said. "Listening to you is like watching a con artist moving shells. Now I see the pea, now I don't."

"If you'll help me—"

"No," Kit said firmly, the police officer in her speaking. "Don't drag me into something about which you're not absolutely positive."

"Only a few pieces aren't in their places," Angie persisted. "The important thing is, we've got to act quickly. Right now!"

"Are you prepared to accuse anyone?" Kit demanded.

Angie struggled for a way around the question. "I'm prepared to go into a home and find the proof, and then accuse a lot of people," she said.

It was Kit's turn to wrestle with her thoughts. She regarded Angie seriously, with a frown that did not waver.

Under Kit's gaze, Angie began to wilt. Her position seemed hopeless, even though she knew she was right.

Then, when everything seemed lost, Kit smiled.

"Angie, Angie," she said. "When you get an idea . . . !" She rose from the table. "I'd better change out of this uniform."

"No, wear it!" Angie begged. "And bring your gun."

"You don't seem to have reasonable cause for entering someone's home. Just a hunch," Kit said.

"It's more than a hunch," Angie responded lamely.

"I'll go with you if you wish," Kit said. "But I have to go as a concerned citizen and not as a police officer. It's illegal to enter someone's home without a warrant. And I have no grounds for a warrant."

Five minutes later Kit's heels rattled on a stretch of bare tile, and then she moved noiselessly over the carpet toward the front door. Six feet tall, she strode in high heels with the same natural, athletic grace that she did in sneakers. Watching her move, Angie was convinced that she could do anything: leap a ten-foot wall or lift the front end of an automobile—or glide deftly across a dance floor.

"Where to?" Kit asked Angie as they got into the car.

"Sixty-third Street," Angie answered. She was trembling slightly. "The number is two thirty-eight."

"Who lives there?"

It required considerable courage to answer. "Mrs. Blanchard," Angie said in a small voice.

Kit leaned back and slapped the steering wheel with both hands. "Angie," she groaned. "Don't do this to me. We've been through all that. Mrs. Blanchard described the man who knocked her out and tore apart her house. He doesn't match your mystery man."

"Mrs. Blanchard lied," Angie said. "The mystery man is over six feet tall, dark-haired, well built, and wore a tan suit. Mrs. Blanchard described a man exactly opposite—short, blond, fat, and wearing a green uniform. She made him as different as she possibly could."

Kit's face expressed hesitation. But it was her last hesitation. After what seemed a crisis of decision making, she put the car in motion.

"We've got to get inside her house," Angie said. "I need time to find the plates Mrs. Blanchard uses to print the money."

"That might take hours," Kit said dubiously.

"It'll take two minutes," Angie replied.

"If you're right."

"I'm right," Angie said, her confidence renewed by Kit's support.

They drove a minute in silence. Then Kit said, "Can you think of an excuse to get past her front door?"

"There are two little neighborhood buddies, Ethel and Patsy," Angie said. "They live across the street and spend their time making up stories about Mrs. Blanchard. They told me she was a witch. Mrs. Blanchard will want to put a stop to such talk."

"It's pretty weak," Kit said uneasily. She had turned down Sixty-third Street and was straining to read the house numbers in the darkness.

"There it is," Angie said. "The one with the two flower pots outside the second-floor window."

Angie studied the house as they walked up the front path. She wouldn't have time to waste on a wrong turn at the top of the stairs.

She thought suddenly of Jess. If only he could be there. He'd never even been aware of the counterfeit ring, and yet he'd been so involved with them. It didn't seem fair to leave him out now, at the ending. But all the clues had slid together so swiftly. There just hadn't been time to bring him back into it.

"Mrs. Blanchard?" Kit said to the lady who opened the door.

"Yes?" She was a frail, white-haired woman with bruises on her face and neck. "What is it?"

"I'm Kit Zane, and this is my sister, Angie. We thought you should know that there is some ugly talk in the neighborhood."

"What kind of talk?"

"People are calling you a witch," Kit said. "We'd like to put a stop to it. May we come in?"

"I'm a witch?" Mrs. Blanchard laughed. "I know

who started that windy-diddy. Ethel and Patsy. Regular little brats, those two."

"May we come in and discuss the girls before we go to their parents?" Kit said.

"The children don't bother me," Mrs. Blanchard said. "They're simply bored around here. They should be off at a summer camp. However, I do appreciate your stopping by."

She moved to close the door.

"One other thing, ma'am," Kit said. "I'm with the Department of Public Safety." She unclasped her handbag and showed her identification.

"A lady policeman? Now, Officer, you mustn't arrest those little girls," Mrs. Blanchard said. "Really, they don't bother me at all."

Kit's tone was clipped and professional when she replied. And her words were a testimony of faith in her little sister.

"We have a report that you are involved with the counterfeiting of twenty-dollar bills."

"Good gracious, however did you come by that?" Mrs. Blanchard said. She seemed genuinely shocked, and to Angie no one had ever looked less guilty or like a criminal than this frail woman.

All at once Angie thought, *What if I'm wrong?* She glanced up at the window on the second floor and remembered what Aunt Velma so often said: "Angie Zane, you can heighten a sneeze into a drama."

Kit said, "Wouldn't you prefer to talk inside?"

Mrs. Blanchard stepped back. "If you wish."

She ushered them into the living room, where Angie and Kit found seats side by side on the sofa. Mrs. Blanchard remained standing, watching them sharply every second.

"We've received this report—"

"Officer," interrupted Mrs. Blanchard. "If you actually believe I'm mixed up with—what did you say?—counterfeiting, you are making a foolish mistake. It will go badly for you."

She wagged a warning finger at Kit and then abruptly changed her manner.

"Look around, my dear," she said sweetly. "I have absolutely nothing to hide. Do I look like a counterfeiter? Search the house. You won't find a printing press or any such silly nonsense. Go ahead. Satisfy yourself."

Angie seized the invitation. Leaving Kit with the burden of manufacturing conversation, she stole quietly up the stairs and turned left into a bedroom. She had to drag over a chair in order to flip the top latches of the window screen.

On the trip downstairs, she made no attempt to muffle her footsteps. She had the proof. In each hand she carried an oilskin bag speckled with dry black dirt. She set set them on the coffee table in front of Kit.

At the sight of the bags, Mrs. Blanchard seemed stricken. She tottered a step. "They're mine! Don't touch them!" she screamed.

Kit motioned the old woman to take a seat and untied one of the bags. She slid out a sheath of cotton bunting. From the bunting she pulled forth a metal plate about six inches long and three inches wide. Within the center oval it bore a picture of Andrew Jackson. In the second oilskin was the plate for printing the other side of the twenty-dollar bill.

"Angie," Kit whispered, balancing the plates in her hands, "how did you know?"

# Chapter
# 12

Kit held the two counterfeit plates as if they were bars of gold. "Angie, how did you ever?" she marveled.

Before Angie could answer, a man spoke. "She's one smart, smart little kitten."

The voice was familiar, and so was the rugged, handsome face. The tall figure seemed to fill the entranceway to Mrs. Blanchard's living room.

It was Angie's omnipresent foe, the mystery man. He stood motionless. Only his lips moved as they widened into a hungry grin. His large, gloved hands hung loosely at his sides like weapons, sheathed but ready.

Mrs. Blanchard sidled a timid step nearer him. "She's a cop. Don't let them get away."

"Shut up," he said scornfully. "There's no way out except the chimney."

His eyes were trained on Kit. He advanced and held out his hand. "The plates."

"They're police property" Kit stated, and dropped them into her handbag.

"The plates," he said, beckoning with his fingers.

"Back off," Kit advised him.

"I've always hankered to know something," he said. "How tough is a lady cop without a gun?"

"We do our job," Kit answered evenly.

He had edged too close. She got up quickly, and they stood measuring each other. Her heels brought her to a height with him.

"You're a big one," he said with a nasty smile.

"Big enough."

"Sparky, too." He grinned approvingly. "But tough enough?"

"You're under arrest," Kit said. "Does that answer your question?"

His hands balled into fists. A look of malicious pleasure settled on his face. He backed to the center of the room and, with a courtly bow, bade her prove herself.

Kit acknowledged the wordless challenge. She gave Angie the handbag and walked around the edge of the coffee table.

Obviously he had no qualms about fighting a woman, or even striking first. But soon to become equally obvious was that he never had come up against a woman like Kit.

His blunder in missing her ear by an eighth of an inch cost him dearly. The blow was thrown while Kit was still taking her stance, and it would have laid her flat.

She reacted instantly, while he was still off balance. She whipped out her arm and snagged his hair, twisting violently. With the other hand she grasped his wrist and bent it behind him.

Most men would have admitted defeat right there. He looked at her with something akin to amusement. Plainly he thought this early advantage a fluke. He lunged sideways, breaking free contemptuously.

He whirled, planting his feet as he spun to face her. She tried a leg sweep. Nimbly he saved himself from falling, but in that split second of concentrating on footwork, he slighted his defense.

A hand chop hacked his neck. A fist drove into the pit of his stomach. He leaned over and was straightened by an uppercut delivered karate-style. He grunted and reeled backward in dumb surprise.

Kit had him hurt, and she stayed relentlessly on the attack. She went after him as if performing an exercise at the police academy. Her every move was deliberate, correct, and efficient. Speed and training were her edge against his weight and muscle.

Eventually, the sum of her blows began to tell. Moment by moment she wore him down, until even his strong body could take no more.

The only fight left in him was empty taunts, which he flung as he stumbled in retreat, all the while glaring at her hatefully. That he was being outfought by a woman had finally penetrated his brain.

Only some tiny reflex of pride enabled him to raise his arm and push out a weak jab. She side-stepped and, mustering her remaining strength, smashed him behind the ear.

The punch put him away. He fell forward stiffly, arms at his sides. On the way down he knocked over an end table and lamp and sent them crashing noisily to the floor.

Kit uttered a high-pitched yelp of relief and gratitude and weariness. She seemed herself on the brink of collapse. "Never again, please," she breathed. "Good grief, he was a ton."

Massaging her right shoulder, she leaned over to make sure of him. He was out cold.

"Let's see who he is, this mystery man of yours, Angie," she said. She dug out his wallet. "The name is Earl Jeeter, and he lives in Denver, Colorado."

With her attention fixed on the wallet, she was caught off guard. The crash that had signaled the end of Earl Jeeter's resistance had also summoned help. The front door opened and a husky man barreled in.

He would have bowled Kit over but for Angie.

She had been clutching the shoulder straps of Kit's handbag throughout the battle, seeking an opportunity to help. Now, as the newcomer charged, she swung the handbag like a hammer thrower.

It smacked him squarely in the belly. The weight of the counterfeit plates inside did the rest. He jackknifed clumsily and landed on the carpet head first, plunging himself into dreamland.

Kit had straightened and was poised on the balls of her feet. "Nice work," she said, her eyes large. She looked down at Earl Jeeter. "He said there was no way out but the chimney. . . . The back door. There must be another—"

With a warning to Mrs. Blanchard to remain where she was, Kit dashed to the rear of the house.

Almost instantly Angie heard the thump of bodies colliding. Someone swore. The voice was too deep to be Kit's. Then the swearing ceased, as if a switch had been thrown. There was a momentary silence, followed by a thud and an immediate wail of pain. The last sound was that of someone making contact with the floor.

"Kit!" Angie screamed. "Are you all right?"

"Yes, stay where you are."

Kit reentered the living room with a passenger. Draped across her shoulders was the luckless guardian of the back door. He lay unsquirming, his eyes closed, and moaned feebly.

Kit said, "He did it all on his own, cracked his head against the door frame. The fight's out of him."

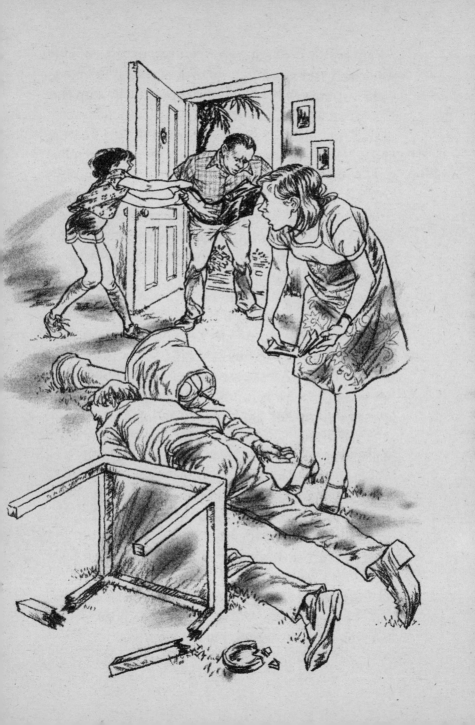

Pausing in the middle of the room, she considered the wreckage and how to deal with it. Kicking aside a splintered chair and lamp, she piled up the victims as though stacking bags of oats. The man on her shoulders she dumped across Earl Jeeter. The jackknife diver she hefted by an arm and a leg and heaved on top of the other two.

"That should do it," she announced.

"Earl Jeeter is the man who followed me," Angie said. "The other two helped him stage the fake killing on the sport fisherman and locked Jess and me in the auto body shop."

Wearily Kit dusted herself and smoothed the creases in her dress. "I'll be up all night filling out the activity report on this," she said. "So before I call in, would you do me a favor?"

"Anything," Angie answered. She would have jumped off the roof for Kit. She had goose bumps from watching her big sister in action.

"Talk to me," Kit said. "Tell me about it—the plates and Mrs. Blanchard and these three."

She gestured at Mrs. Blanchard and the heap of senseless men. "Is there anyone else involved?"

"One more, at least," Angie replied. "But you can find him without any trouble." She tilted her head toward the spidery tangle of arms and legs. "Shouldn't we tie them?"

"I doubt they'll feel very frisky for a while," Kit said. Nevertheless, she walked to Mrs. Blanchard. "Do you have any rope, ma'am? *Strong* rope."

Mrs. Blanchard turned her face away and didn't reply.

"Look in the kitchen and garage," Kit instructed Angie. "I'll watch our sleeping beauties."

Angie searched the kitchen, but found only a ball of thin twine in one of the cupboards. She had better luck in the garage. Hanging from a pegboard above the washing machine were two electric extension cords and several lengths of old chain. She took them to Kit.

The men had recovered their senses. Angie was afraid she might have to quiet them with the handbag while they were being trussed.

She was mistaken. They were perfect lambs. Ending up like discarded baggage had tamed them wonderfully — and altered some ancient male beliefs.

*They'll probably never be the same,* Angie thought.

Kit arranged the men to her liking and shooed Angie into the dining room. There they could speak in relative privacy and at the same time watch the men and Mrs. Blanchard across the foyer.

"Comfortable?" Kit asked.

"Comfortable," Angie answered.

"Now humor me," Kit said. "Tell me what in heaven's name is going on."

# Chapter
# 13

"**B**egin with the number three," Kit said. "When Aunt Velma said *three* at the dinner table this evening, you practically leaped from the chair."

"I remembered something *you* told me—Mrs. Blanchard has lived in this house for three years," Angie said. "And then I thought of Frank Congdon, who stole the pens from Mr. Wells's garage. And, of course, the mystery man, Earl Jeeter. He had the wrong house. And the white van that—"

"Whoa!" Kit exclaimed. "Take it slowly."

Angie paused to organize her thoughts. The pieces were flying around in her head. She had to sort them out and fit them in line.

Once she had them all in place, she said, "Earl Jeeter was hired to get the plates for the counterfeit twenty-dollar bills from Mrs. Blanchard. Do

you recall writing down the address of the Weygand house when the Wolfpack robbed it?"

"I left the paper on your desk."

"You scribbled," Angie said. "I couldn't make
out whether the last number was a seven or a one.
Then I realized Earl Jeeter had run into the same
problem with a three and an eight. The address of
Mrs. Blanchard's house is two thirty-eight on
Sixty-*third* Street. He misread the address written down for him as Sixty-*eighth* Street."

"And he ended up at Sergeant Casey's house?"
Kit said.

Angie nodded. "Jess and I saw him there, and he
saw us. I had no idea what he was really doing. I
just thought he acted suspiciously."

"You said he spun his car in a U-turn to get away
from you."

"He burned rubber," Angie said. "Later that
same morning he realized that he'd mistaken the
number three for an eight and went to Sixty-third
Street. He got into Mrs. Blanchard's house by pretending he was selling cleaning fluid."

"You had that part right from the beginning,"
Kit said.

"Mrs. Blanchard wouldn't tell him where she
had hidden the plates," Angie continued. "She was
afraid he might kill her once he knew. He tried
beating it out of her. When that didn't do any good,
he tied her up and tore her house inside out. He
didn't find the plates because he looked in the
wrong places."

"If I understand you, Mrs. Blanchard didn't dare tell the police the truth," Kit said. "She had to make it appear like an ordinary robbery. Fine. She made up a man in a green uniform who looked nothing like Earl Jeeter. Fine again. But I still don't know how the number three ties in."

"You told me that Mrs. Blanchard was a widow," Angie replied, "and that she moved into her house three years ago."

"Well?"

"Three was the very first connection," Angie said. "Frank Congdon said that Mr. Wells, who owns the convenience store, had his sister living with him until three years ago. That's when Mrs. Blanchard moved into her house. Mr. Wells was left alone—"

"Hold on," Kit interrupted. "Who is Frank Congdon?"

"A boy Jess and I caught stealing from Mr. Wells," Angie explained. "He had taken some cheap pens. It was kind of a hobby with him. He said Mr. Wells went away for a few days every two or three months, leaving the house empty. That's when he would slip into the garage."

"You mean the house."

"No, the garage," Angie said. "It was filled with all sorts of inexpensive stuff, like bulbs and bars of soap and combs."

"How strange," said Kit. "With a storeroom in the back of his store, why does Mr. Wells need to use his garage?"

"That's the point," Angie said. "The merchandise in his garage was never meant to be sold at the store. It would foul up his bookkeeping, for one thing. Everything in the garage was for his own private use."

"A garage full of light bulbs and combs and whatnot?" Kit declared. "He couldn't use it all in one lifetime. Angie, that's downright silly."

"Let me tell you about the day Earl Jeeter followed me," Angie answered patiently. "I told you I ducked into Mr. Wells's store to escape, and I sneaked out the back. But what I didn't mention—because I didn't think it was important then—was that to reach the rear exit, I had to pass through the storeroom. Most of the shelves were half empty. Why didn't he fill them from his garage?"

"All right," Kit said. "So the merchandise in the garage wasn't intended for the store. What's the harm of hoarding? It's foolish, but hardly unlawful."

"Not if you understand what he was really doing," Angie said. "Mr. Wells makes those out-of-town trips for a reason—*to pass counterfeit money.*"

"Angie, now really!" Kit objected. "You can't accuse him because he's a hoarder, even if it turns out he is Mrs. Blanchard's brother. I agree about a connection. His sister moved out three years ago, at the same time that Mrs. Blanchard moved into this house. But he's a fine man. Everyone likes him."

"Think of it this way," Angie said. "Mr. Wells

drives to other cities. He buys small items, things costing a dollar or two. He pays for each item with a counterfeit twenty and receives his change in good money."

"You're assuming," Kit said. "A lot of people leave Dadesville on trips. Does that make them counterfeiters? "

"Add something else," Angie said. "Mr. Wells is a storekeeper and therefore hates to see good merchandise wasted. Suppose, to boot, he is a miser."

"You lost me," Kit confessed.

"The small things he buys out of town with counterfeit money he *keeps*. He can't bring himself to throw them away or give them away. He puts them in his garage, where he thinks they'll be safe and he can use them himself. Make sense?"

Kit's attitude underwent a change. She sat very still. "Go on," she said.

"Mr. Wells might never have been found out except that Jess and I stumbled on Frank Congdon stealing pens," Angie said. "And the very same morning, the Wolfpack robbed the Weygand house."

"Don't tell me those teenagers were working with the counterfeiters!"

Angie shook her head. "They just threw a whale of a scare into Mr. Wells. It was the first time the Wolfpack had struck on Seaward Island. Because they always brag to the police after each robbery, he couldn't afford to delay. If they robbed his house, he'd have police all over him, investigating, asking questions. How could he explain a garage full of merchandise?"

Angie took a second to make sure she had everything laid out properly in her mind. Then she plunged on.

"Mr. Wells had to get the stuff out of his garage fast," she said. "He loaded everything into a white Chevy van that he probably got from the crooked auto body shop, Donovan's. The problem was to get it off the island without being seen. Remember, he lives near the Sixty-eighth Street Bridge, which is closed. He had to drive almost the entire length of the island to the Whitehorse Bridge."

Kit said, "Why didn't he wait and drive off at night, after everyone had gone to sleep?"

"Uh-huh. He knew, as you once told me, that the police don't patrol Seaward Island on weekdays. But occasionally the police do check there at night. He couldn't risk meeting a police car. He'd be stopped. The police would want to know what a delivery van was doing on an island with no stores, and after business hours."

"He could easily have talked his way out of that situation," Kit said. "After all, he does live on the island. And he could have pretended the bulbs and combs and things were for his store."

"Maybe, and maybe not," Angie said. "Anyway, everything he did suggests how scared he was. He probably even hired a driver. I'd say Mr. Wells had gone off the island before the van started its drive. He was ready to skip town if anything went wrong."

"That may be," Kit said. "But a lot of people must have seen the van."

"Everyone saw it, but no one paid it any attention," Angie said, "because all eyes were on the boat."

"The sport fisherman?"

"Yes. Mr. Wells had Earl Jeeter and the other two men steal it. They were in contact with the van, and they timed the boat's run and the fake shootings along the coast to match the van's progress."

Kit crinkled her nose. "Sounds like a great deal of trouble just to get rid of some things like bulbs and soap."

"The stuff in his garage wasn't all he had to move," Angie said. "Don't forget the counterfeit bills. If the Wolfpack found them, he'd be finished. There must have been a pile of the phony twenties —too many for the trunk of his car."

"If that was the case, the van was necessary," Kit agreed. "He must really have been in a panic."

"He was," Angie said. "But in case anything happened with the boat, he had protected himself in another way. Jess and I noticed the van. Jess saw it from the front and thought it was a three-year-old Chevy. I saw it from the rear and thought it was a Ford, like Uncle Bert's. "

"You're saying Mr. Wells had one end altered?"

"Probably at Donovan's body shop," Angie said. "There was a white van in a stall when Jess and I were locked up there. I'd say it was being restored to its original condition."

"That's really quite brilliant," Kit said. "Witnesses who noticed the van would be at odds over whether it was a Chevy or a Ford. So their testimony would be discounted."

"Jess and I searched for the sport fisherman," Angie resumed. "We found it, and Earl Jeeter found us. Can you imagine what he must have thought when he saw me by the boat? He had seen me near Sergeant Casey's house. He had seen me in front of Mrs. Blanchard's house, which, obviously, he'd been watching for Mr. Wells, just as he was tonight. And he'd seen me go into Mr. Wells's store!"

Kit grinned. "He must have thought you were a one-girl FBI."

"I must have driven him bananas," Angie crowed.

She paused. She had come to the parts that required her special ability—imagination.

"As I see it," she said, "Mr. Wells and his sister, Mrs. Blanchard, could have had a major argument. Mr. Wells could have ordered her out of the house, and she left, taking the plates with her. More likely, though, he bought this house for her and gave her the plates for safekeeping. Either way, she couldn't tell the police the truth about the attack by Earl Jeeter. She was involved too deeply."

"If Mr. Wells trusted her with the plates, why did he have to send Earl Jeeter to get them back?" Kit asked. "Wouldn't she have returned them willingly?"

"In the beginning, yes," Angie said. "But after a while, the plates must have got to Mrs. Blanchard. At first she probably printed one or two bills a month and spent them right here in Dadesville. Then she must have become bolder. Four or five bills started showing up in a week. You told me that. Mr. Wells must have been furious. I guess he demanded she give the plates back. When she refused, he hired Earl Jeeter and those other two."

"There must be a printing press somewhere in this house," Kit said thoughtfully.

"No," Angie disagreed. "Mrs. Blanchard is too clever. She and Mr. Wells have a sister, her only regular visitor, according to neighbors. I'd guess the sister has a hand press at her home and a very good excuse for owning it."

"Stop right there!" Kit cried, springing from her chair.

Angie was startled, until she saw Mrs. Blanchard in the foyer. The woman had slipped into the living room and was close to the front door. She glowered at Kit, but retreated meekly to her seat.

Kit's cry had aroused the three bound men. They whined. She had slung them over the back of the sofa, heads resting on the cushions. Now they kicked their legs and moaned loudly, discomforted by stiffening joints and sore stomach muscles.

Kit marched over to them. "Here, I'll make you comfortable." She lifted them one after the other and laid them gently on the carpet, side by side.

"I'd better call the station," she said to Angie. "Watch them. If anyone twitches a finger, holler."

She was gone a full five minutes.

"Oh, brother!" she remarked on her return. "You should have heard the captain. He's mad as a bear that we took on those three ourselves. He's sending help."

"Help?" Angie squeaked. "Does it look like we need help?"

Kit beamed. "We do make a pretty good pair, don't we?"

She took out a comb and ran it through her short blond hair with quick, tugging strokes. Suddenly she pulled the comb free. Her cheeks reddened. "Angie, I never learned how you found the plates!"

"The two girls across the street, Ethel and Patsy, put me on to it," Angie answered. "They said Mrs. Blanchard never pours water into the two flower pots outside her window. She just replaces the flowers as they die. So I got to thinking. Why? Once I had the question, the answer practically jumped into my lap. You see—"

"Let me take it from there," Kit broke in. "Mrs. Blanchard didn't care about the flowers. They were just a cover. She was afraid water might ruin the plates, which she'd hidden in the flower pots!"

Success, Angie decided right there, was everything it was cracked up to be. Kit's face was the reward for the long, dull weeks of jogging and the dangers of the past two days.

The patrol cars rolled up with sirens lashing the air and blinkers lighting the street with flashing streaks of red and blue and amber. Before dawn, Mr. Wells would be under arrest and Angie's assessment would prove correct in almost every detail.

At the station the sisters became separated. Angie saw the captain patting Kit's back as they disappeared into his office.

A big sergeant plunked Angie onto a table in the center of the detectives' room. The men made her tell over and over how Kit had tamed Earl Jeeter and his henchmen.

Around midnight she and Kit related the story once more to a reporter. The woman asked about Angie's grades at school and made her pose feeling Kit's muscle for the photographer. At one o'clock the mobile TV unit arrived. A lieutenant had to give his solemn word before the commentator became convinced. It was no hoax. Angie Zane, age twelve, who had helped capture the Wolfpack, had also aided her sister in the capture of the counterfeit ring. All in less than twenty-four hours.

With the many interruptions, it was close to

three o'clock in the morning before Kit finished her verbal report and her paperwork. The two sisters drove home.

"If I know Aunt Velma, she'll be sitting up in her armchair fast asleep," Angie said. "We'll have to lick those guys one more time."

"We can make it a party," Kit said. "We never did get around to the celebration cake at dinner."

Angie felt like staying up all night and eating cake till there was nothing left but crumbs. But, no, that wouldn't be fair. She had to save a big slice for Jess.

## About the Author

Donald Sobol has written more than fifty books during the last twenty-five years. Among these are the enormously popular *Encyclopedia Brown* mysteries. Two of these, *Encyclopedia Brown Carries On* and *Encyclopedia Brown and the Case of the Dead Eagles*, are now available in Apple Paperback editions.
Mr. Sobol grew up in New York City and now lives in Florida with his family.